EMBATTLED MINDS

BY
J.M. MADDEN

Acknowledgements

As always, I have to thank my husband for never doubting I could do what I said I would. I love you dearly.

To my parents for their unwavering faith and support. I love you!

Donna and Robyn, you guys are kick ass critique partners and friends. I couldn't have done this without you. Bruce, thank you for your unwavering belief in this series.

Madden Militia, you ladies are awesome! Thank you for prodding me on and loving my guys. Your excitement feeds mine!

To Mary Y., Rebekah W., Suzie H., Denise S., Jeanette P., Becky C. thank you for being Super Beta Readers!

And to our military, I sincerely thank you for everything that you do. You've taken on a job that very few could handle, but you've done it well. You have my deepest appreciation.

To military families, I admire you more than I can ever articulate. Thank you for being the support they need.

A NOTE FROM THE AUTHOR

Several years ago, the government hired a private research firm to study PTSD and the returning soldier. The RAND report was completed and published in 2008, and if you would like to read the report in it's entirety, you can go to this link:

http://www.rand.org/content/dam/rand/pubs/monographs/2008/RAND_MG720.pdf

I've listed some startling highlights below. Information is attributed to their report, unless attributed otherwise.

Mind you, now, these numbers are several years old, and actually tracking PTSD is a difficult job in itself. Not all veterans who left Iraq and Afghanistan suffered from the symptoms of PTSD *at that time*, but it developed later on down the road. The government is also notoriously bad about keeping track of its veterans. If the veteran refused treatment, there's no way to track them.

~Almost 3 million American veterans have returned from service in Iraq and Afghanistan, and at least 20% of them have PTSD and/or depression. I, personally, assume these are conservative estimates, because the data is five years old. But, if it is correct, a minimum of

600,000 veterans have a varying degree of PTSD and/or depression. The report I read stated that the incidence of PTSD was magnified if the veteran also had a Traumatic Brain Injury (TBI).

~50% of the veterans that did show signs of PTSD refused treatment, and of those that *did* accept treatment, only half of them get 'minimally adequate' treatment. In other words, if they did ask for help, they didn't get proper help. So, from a veterans point of view, this would be extremely frustrating.

~In 2008, suicide deaths began to surpass combat related fatalities. It is reported that on average, 5 active duty personnel attempt suicide each day. (ptsdusa.org)

One of my characters in Embattled Minds is a Vietnam veteran, created when I found this information at veteransandptsd.com:

~Back in the 1980's, the government commissioned the National Vietnam Veterans Readjustment Study, and found that only 15% of Vietnam vets had ptsd symptoms at that time. But when they did a reanalysis in 2003, that number had inflated to 80%, or 4 out of every 5 vets!

That number is staggering to me, because there are/were 8.2 million veterans from the 'Vietnam Era', those that served any where at any time during Vietnam. To imagine that potentially millions of people suffer from PTSD in our country right now saddens me. The fact that we don't have comprehensive help for them pisses me off.

That's why, with this book, I'm going to make a donation to the Beck Institute of Cognitive Behavioral Therapy (http://www.soldierssuicideprevention.org/), outside Philadelphia. They offer scholarships to medical personnel training to deal with active duty and veteran military service members struggling with suicidal thoughts, post traumatic stress disorder, depression, substance abuse, anger, anxiety and other behavioral issues.

If a soldier/Marine wants competent treatment, it should be available. Period.

So, thank you for reading and supporting.

~~~~If you haven't read Embattled Road (free at all outlets) or Embattled Hearts, I strongly suggest you do. And be sure to read to the end for an excerpt from Embattled Home, Chad's story, out now!

Happy Reading!

CHAPTER ONE

EMBER NORTON LOOKED up at the sound of the front door of the Frog Dog Grill opening and closing, and tried not to be disappointed that it wasn't the group of Marines she'd been serving for the past few weeks. At least she thought they were Marines. There was a certain way they carried themselves, as if they were badasses but didn't need to flaunt it like the younger, less-experienced soldiers.

Every Saturday they came in, like clockwork. Seven o'clock. She'd gotten used to their mismatched mugs and quiet humor, not to mention their powerful personalities.

Who was she kidding? There was only one guy she actively looked for. The massive Viking that made everybody else look like a child.

His name was Zeke. Built like a brick shithouse, as her dad would say, he drew every gaze when he strode into the place, dominating the room. The women drooled over his massive chest, cobbled stomach and lean hips, until they saw his face, then their interest turned to pity. It was disgusting to watch, because they sometimes couldn't hide their reactions quickly enough for him not to see.

Ember didn't know what had happened to him, but

he appeared to have been beaten or tortured to within an inch of his life. Deep, brutal scars traced over his forehead and down his neck. She assumed he'd been injured in the war.

Dark blond hair with a hint of curl hid his eyes. She'd managed to see him fully a few times, and each glimpse made her want to see more. She wasn't one of the ones turned off by his looks. Ember knew she'd never met him, but he seemed familiar to her. It was as if they'd connected long ago, before the scars, then lost touch.

Some of his wounds were deep and still looked angry and painful. Others were just faint white tracings across his skin. It looked like his face had been shattered into about six pieces, then stitched back together by a drunken surgeon. One deep line bisected his forehead diagonally, slid down to run below his left brow then toward his ear. Another, lighter one, nipped the edge of his bottom lip, tugging it out of symmetry when he smiled. It curled down his chin and into his darker blond beard. She felt sure he wore the beard to hide more marks.

She would have been intimidated by his harsh looks if she hadn't caught the blazing awareness shining from his stunning, thickly lashed, ice-blue eyes.

The Frog Dog was located in a busy shopping center. Soldiers came in to relax often. They loved the military memorabilia her father had lined the walls and hung the ceiling with. For the most part she'd gotten used to the testosterone she had to wade through every night. But Zeke didn't overwhelm her with his masculinity. Though he was huge, at least six and a half feet tall—largest in his group—the way he slouched in the chair and let his hair fall forward to hide his face almost made him seem smaller. The only time he'd frightened her had been the night several weeks ago when he'd kicked those frat boys out.

A drunk had grabbed her ass and she'd cried out, surprised more than anything. Almost immediately, Zeke had appeared at her side. The scars on his face stood out white against his red skin as he confronted that group, and there'd been zero give in his expression or his shiver-inducing baritone. The set of his jaw and the angle of his massive shoulders told everybody in the bar he wasn't going to tolerate that kind of treatment of her.

Once again, her heart thudded at the way he'd protected her. Nobody had ever done anything like that for her before. They'd been trading skin-prickling glances ever since then.

She ran the bar rag over the glass in her hand and set it on the lower ledge, easy to grab for the next drink. It was quiet today. Surprisingly so, considering it was the middle of the month and almost Christmas. But, it was early afternoon. The shopping crowd would be rolling in soon, thirsty and hungry.

She glanced at the black apron hanging on the peg by the swing-through kitchen door. She wondered if her dad would come in tonight. He'd been gone too long.

One of the waitresses called her name, and she turned away with a sigh. She had too much to do to be mopin'.

ZEKE LOOKED FOR and found Ember as soon as he cleared the doorway into the shadowed bar and grill. She stood across the room, smiling her big smile and pointing something out in the menu to a customer. Her long, almost-black hair hung over her shoulder in a long braid. The man warmed to her, and even from across the room Zeke could see his interest. Ember seemed friendly, but oblivious to the edge that had crept into the man's smile as his gaze wandered down her form.

Ducking his head, he followed the guys across the room. The table they normally sat at was full, so they had to settle into one nearer the bar. The proximity to the other patrons was a little much. Diego looked twitchy, like he'd rather leave than have his back to people. He adjusted his eyepatch.

Chad grinned at the guy, always the peacemaker. "Just one beer, then we can bug out if it's too much."

Diego gave a tight nod, and with a final look behind him to map out targets, he took off his coat and settled into the chair, hands below the table. Zeke knew he probably already had a knife in his hands. Seemed like they all carried knives in their pockets anymore, just to have some sense of security. Terrell shook his head and settled across from Chad, tipping back on two legs.

Ember scrawled something on her pad and headed for the kitchen. As if she felt him watching, she glanced around and immediately locked gazes with him. She smiled and threw a little wave.

Zeke swallowed heavily and turned to look down at the table, his skin tightening uncomfortably across his scalp. The scars there didn't move the way regular skin did, and when he got embarrassed, which seemed like all the time, it felt like ants biting at him. He took a heavy breath and started lining up his words in his head, because he knew she would be over for their order.

No sooner had the thought occurred and she was there, smiling big and planting one hand on her curvy hip. "Hi guys. What can I get you?"

Chad knew to lead off, because it gave Zeke time. Diego unclenched his jaw enough to order his cola, and Terrell ordered a house beer. Then, she turned her big, dark chocolate colored eyes to him.

He took a breath, thought about the words and spit them out.

Her fine dark brows furrowed and she cocked her head. "Uh, what?"

Fighting not to flinch from her look, he replayed the words in his head. Oh, no. He hadn't said dark chocolate eyes, had he? He glanced at the guys and they were all grinning at him, and he knew he had. *Fuck!*

"House beer," he snapped.

With a curious look, she turned away.

"Did I…a-actually say d-dark chocolate eyes?"

Chad laughed out loud and clapped him on the shoulder. "I knew you liked the girl, but I didn't expect you to hit on her like that."

Zeke shook his head, totally disgusted and complete-ly mortified. As if it weren't bad enough he couldn't talk like a normal human being, now his brain had to pick up words he had no intention of uttering? It had tricked him before, but never so brilliantly.

For the millionth time, he wished he'd never taken cover behind that wall.

Within a few minutes she brought their drinks and asked about food. When the attention turned to him, he stabbed a finger at the menu and didn't say a word. She grinned and scribbled his preference, then turned away.

Once the distraction Ember brought with her disappeared, they shifted in their seats, uncomfortable with being in the middle of the crowded bar. The hair lifted on the back of his neck. Zeke glanced around and more than one patron's gaze shifted away guiltily, unwilling to acknowledge them. That's what pissed him off more than anything. If they had questions, he would much rather they just come up and ask than whisper behind their hands and sneak glances at him. He knew he was fugly. He was surprised nobody had said it out loud yet.

The beer in front of him began to slosh and he looked across at Diego. His buddy jogged his leg beneath the table, unable to control his anxiety. *Uh, oh.* Chad recognized the impending disaster as well, because he pushed to his feet. "Mr. Ortiz, outside! I've got something in my truck to show you, man."

Diego's glazed dark eye focused in on his boss, and he nodded. Terrell caught his chair as Diego shoved to his feet and lurched toward the door. Zeke hoped nobody noticed the blade hidden in his hand against his hip. He pushed to his feet as well, grabbing his coat from the seat-back.

"I... b-better go t-too."

Terrell nodded and leaned back in his chair. "I'll keep our seats."

Zeke navigated through the rapidly filling room, hoping that nobody reached out to Diego, because it would be hard to tell what the recently discharged Marine would do. Once out in the parking lot, he followed the men toward Chad's bright red truck at the far end of the lot. Chad had just dropped the tailgate and was talking to Diego about some horse he was thinking about buying. Just making noise to keep the other man grounded. Diego paced through the snow, trampling it beneath his boots, oblivious to everything around him. The open blade in his hand swished back and forth against the side of his jeans.

Zeke sat on the tailgate beside Chad, zipping his coat around him. Diego had left his inside, but with sweat beading his brow, he seemed to be too hot to notice.

They sat there in the cold for the better part of twenty minutes as Diego fought demons only he could see. Eventually, he slowed and looked at the muddy path he'd made in the snow, frowning heavily. He stopped in front of them, scowling. "Kind of went off the deep end, huh?"

Zeke shook his head. "Nah. No biggie."

Chad reached out and punched the sweating man in the arm. "Newbie. You gotta get your shit under control, man. You're signed up for counseling, right?"

Diego nodded. "I am, but it'll be months before I'll

be able to get in. They already told me that."

Chad crossed his arms over his chest. "Then we'll see if we can find you another counselor in the meantime. We've all been there, and still have issues to varying degrees. It'll ease, I promise you. But it takes time." He shrugged, tugging his jacket tighter around himself and pulling a butterscotch from his pocket. "When you feel it coming on like that, you need to get out of Dodge. Don't try to tough it out. Especially in a group of civvies like that."

Diego nodded, and looked out over the parking lot. "I didn't know it was going to be that bad until I had my knife in my hand."

He looked down at the wicked desert camo'ed lock blade in his palm. With one thumb, he closed the blade and tucked it into the corner of his jeans pocket.

Zeke chuckled when he caught sight of his buddy's pants. "You can't d-do that too...o-often."

Diego looked down at his hip and choked out a laugh. Where the blade had run over and over again, the jean had worn through to the heavier threads. It looked like a couple years worth of wear had taken place just in one six-inch spot. "Damn."

"Zeke, why don't you go in and see if Ember can box up our meals. We'll go to my apartment or something."

Swallowing, his heart jerked in his chest. Chad wanted *him* to go in and talk to her?

Diego shook his dark head. "Nah, I'm okay Sergeant. Go on in and eat your food. Bring mine out when you're done."

"Yeah, right."

Chad's phone buzzed in his pocket. He tapped the screen and the illumination lit his face. "Terrell has our regular seats."

Diego pursed his lips and glanced around, then readjusted the eyepatch over his right eye. "I think I can go in, if I can have my back to the wall."

Chad folded his arms again and surveyed the other man. "Are you sure? We can't have an incident."

Nodding, Diego gave Chad good eyecontact. "I can, Boss Man. I won't go off on these civvies."

He smirked, as if the mere thought was ridiculous. And in actuality, it probably was. Diego Ortiz was one of the best security men Zeke had ever seen work, hands down. The missing eye messed with his depth perception a little bit, but not enough to keep him from doing his job.

Zeke wrapped his arm around Diego's neck, tugging him into a brotherly hug. "Come on, dude. My beer's...g-getting warm."

They trailed back into the restaurant, Chad in front and Zeke covering Diego's back. As soon as he walked in, Ember's curvy shape caught his eye, disappearing through the swinging kitchen door at the back of the restaurant.

Terrell grinned as they resettled at the shadowed table farthest from the bar. "Find anything good out there in the snow?"

"Hell, no," Diego muttered.

Having the wall at his back immediately seemed to put him at ease. Zeke was glad Diego had been able to control his anxiety. Integrating into crowds was one of the most difficult things to deal with when they came back home.

A plate thumped down in front of him, and when he glanced up, he was eye level with Ember's plump breasts in the white Frog Dog T-shirt. Awareness skittered through his body, settling in his groin. She turned and set Terrell's plate in front of him, then the other two. When she was done, she quite naturally rested her hand on Zeke's shoulder. He fought not to tense up like a Motherfucker.

"I kept it warm until you got back, but if it doesn't taste right let me know and I'll get you a new order. Is there anything else you need?"

They all shook their heads and she faded away through the crowd.

He drew a deep breath and then another, fighting the draw to her that would never be satisfied. Deliberately, he picked up his sandwich. Perfect, as always.

"That was nice she kept it warm for us," Chad murmured.

They all nodded. Nothing else was said as they plowed through the food. Ember paused long enough to make sure everything was okay and drop off another round of drinks, then she was on the run again. The crowd picked up and once again it seemed like they were short handed. When he finished with his meal, he made sure to police his trash and mess so that she didn't have to, piling it all on the plate. Then, nursing his fresh beer, he turned his chair enough to pretend to watch the giant flatscreen over the bar. In actuality, he watched Ember. She was more fascinating to him than anything on TV.

Eager to laugh, she charmed the customers with her wit and personality. The women seemed to sense that she wasn't a threat to their men, even though the men watched her curvy ass whenever they thought they could get away with it.

There seemed to be a tiredness to her today, as if something weighed on her mind. More than once she glanced at the kitchen door, as if waiting for somebody to come through it. She didn't wear a wedding band, so he knew she wasn't married, but maybe she was involved with someone. The cook, maybe?

Aggravation tightened the muscles across his chest as his ever-helpful mind flashed pictures of her locked in an embrace with some unknown man. He wanted to beat the shit out of him, whoever he was.

More than once, she glanced at him and caught him staring, but he couldn't force himself to look away. He wanted her to sit down and talk to them, but he didn't want to see the disgust on her face as he tried to speak. Maybe it wouldn't play out the way he thought it would. She'd never been anything *but* kind to all of them.

He didn't force himself to come in here every week for her kindness, though.

The crowd finally began to thin, and the next time she swung around with fresh drinks, Chad pulled out an empty chair from the table beside theirs and held his hand out in invitation. She seemed surprised, but grateful as she sank down onto the seat. Zeke could have kissed his meddling buddy, and cursed him. Every muscle in his body tightened as her heat invaded his space.

"Oh, that hurts so good." She arched her feet and wiggled her ankles. "Thank you. I needed a break."

"You need to delegate," Chad told her bluntly. "It seems like you do seventy-five percent of the work in here, though there are other people working."

Ember winced and looked around. The other waitresses were busy, but still managed to stop and talk. "You're right, I know. But I'm managing tonight. I have to cover all the holes."

Chad shook his head, grinning. "No, you have to manage what you have. You can't do that running around trying to put out every fire. You need to park yourself and direct."

She smiled and Zeke caught his breath. This close he could see every pore in her smooth skin, and her dark brown eyes had golden flecks in them that sparkled when she smiled. Her dark bangs curled over her forehead to rest on her brow, damp at the temples. "Like the military?"

Chad smiled and nodded. "It's worked very well for hundreds of years. You should try it."

Her eyes dimmed. "My dad tells me the same thing, but I feel bad when I tell people what to do. It's just not my style. Are you guys all military?"

Zeke nodded. "Former."

Her gaze swung in his direction. One lone finger

reached out and teased at the edge of his straining T-shirt sleeve, tracing the bottom of the anchor, globe and eagle tattoo. "Are all of you Marines?"

Goose bumps pebbled his skin from her gentle touch, and his jaw ached from being clenched. His dick hardened painfully as her fingers drifted away, and he shifted in his chair. She switched her attention to the other three at the table before she could see his reaction.

Chad nodded, but Terrell grimaced. "You couldn't pay me to be a jarhead. Navy."

She grinned at Terrell. "I have a cousin in the Navy. She loves it."

He winked at her and rocked back in his chair.

"Best place to be."

They all laughed and disagreed, but it was what they'd done many times before.

Ember laughed along with them. "Looks like you're in the minority, here." Terrell shrugged and continued to smile, content.

EMBER REALIZED AS she sat there that she really liked these guys. They were thoughtful and kind, and weren't talking to her just to get into her pants. She wanted to touch Zeke again. Feel that power beneath her hand. "So, what do you guys do now? Other than hang out in my restaurant every Saturday night?"

Chad, the cute one with sharp blue eyes and Texas twang in his voice, leaned forward. "We run an all-veteran investigative service, and provide corporate and personal security."

Ember raised her brows, genuinely surprised. "Really? That's interesting. My dad's a former Marine and worked for a while at Denver PD. He'd probably like to meet you. He's part owner of this place, but he's not here tonight. Maybe some other time he can have a drink with you."

"We'd be honored."

"I'll let him know when he comes back," she promised. "He loves meeting other vets. It's why he bought this restaurant. He wanted a place he and his buddies could be comfortable in. The guys from his company all come out once a year just to hang and reminisce."

She smiled sadly. "Unfortunately, that's kind of why he's been off for the past few nights. One of his good friends took his own life last week."

The men fell silent, then Chad offered their condolences. She shrugged. "I didn't know him, but it's really tearing my dad up. He hasn't been sleeping or eating right, and he's been off work for several days now."

She was afraid to tell them that she lived in fear that she would go home one night and find he'd done the same thing.

No, he's taking care of Drew. He wouldn't do that in front of his grandson.

CHAPTER TWO

D UNCAN GLANCED AT his ringing cellphone on the floor beside the weight bench, but didn't recognize the number. If it was important, they'd leave a message. He continued to butterfly the forty pound weights, working his pectorals. The burn felt good. He'd gotten out of the habit of exercising the way he used to, and his body was starting to show it. Just going a tad soft around the middle, a little less cut. But that little bit of definition he was losing now would be five times harder to put back on than it used to be.

Damn, it sucked getting old.

Preston punched a weight bag hanging from the corner ceiling, and didn't even seem to be breathing hard. But then, Duncan had twelve or thirteen years on him.

Chad pounded along on the treadmill, steel blade on his left leg flashing. He seemed to be faster now than before he lost his leg, years ago.

His back twinged as he rolled to a sitting position, and his hip popped, painfully. He'd have to use the Jacuzzi tonight when he got home. If he didn't, he'd be stiff as a board tomorrow. Pushing to his feet, he carried the weights to the rack against the wall and dropped them into place.

"Hey, Dunc, you seen Palmer today?" Chad gasped out.

Duncan swiped his face with a towel as he walked to the treadmill.

"No, not today. He said he'd be in tomorrow for a while, but he's looking for a gift for Shannon."

Chad grinned and glanced at him. "She's got him so pussy-whipped."

A half-full bottle of water hit Chad high on his back, jolting him off stride. Only natural athleticism kept him from landing in a heap at the bottom of the treadmill. He slapped the red button on the console and looked around.

"Fuck you, Lowell."

Chad laughed when he saw Gunny Palmer sitting in his sport chair a few feet away, dressed in workout clothes.

"Well, you are. Did I see you carrying her fabulous, bejewelled purple purse the other day?"

Palmer clamped his heavy jaw, dark eyes narrowing. "Yes, you did. I'll carry the damn thing everywhere she goes if she wants me to. You know why?"

"Why?" Chad asked, laughing.

"Because I get to go home and crawl into bed with her at the end of the day. And if she's fucking happy, so am I."

Duncan punched Chad on the shoulder. "I think he's got a point."

Chad flipped them both the bird and headed for the

bathroom at the far end of the room. He turned before he left, though, and smiled. "I am happy for you, Gunny. You two are perfect for each other."

Palmer nodded once. "Thanks, Chad."

Duncan looked at his second in command of the company. John Palmer used to be a sour, uncooperative SOB. Over the past few weeks, ever since he'd been with Shannon, he'd changed. Easier to talk to without getting your head chewed off, more instructive with the younger guys. All around a better guy.

"I, personally, thought you looked fine with the purse."

John glared, then burst out laughing. "You're not right in the head, fucker."

Duncan grinned, glad that his buddy had found his piece of heaven. If Palmer could do it, it gave him hope that he wasn't a lost cause. "Seems late for you to be here."

"Shannon's parents are parked in the driveway till after Christmas. House is getting small."

Laughing, Duncan followed John to the weight bench he himself had just vacated. The other man shifted from the chair easily, and Duncan handed him the fifty pound weights he preferred from the rack. Preston continued to pound the bag in the corner of the room. He'd given no indication that he'd even heard the joking between the partners, though Duncan had no doubt the man knew everything that went on.

John settled to his back and started doing compressions, barely even slowing down for the substantial weight. "I have to find her a gift and I have no idea what she wants."

Duncan frowned. "I don't know that I can help you out with that, buddy."

"You don't have any ideas at all?"

"Well," he sighed. "She likes purses, and animals."

John was shaking his head. "We already have Pickle and Gray Cat. I about had a heart-attack the other morning when I ran over Gray Cat's tail. She screamed and I about pissed my pants."

Duncan laughed at the visual.

"Well, you could always get her jewelry. An engagement ring, perhaps?"

One of the weights slipped in Palmer's hand and Duncan lunged for it, but the Gunny caught it himself.

"Are you crazy? It's only been a month since I moved in with her."

Duncan shrugged. "Okay. It was just a thought."

But the suggestion had been planted. He could almost hear the wheels in John's head turning. As he walked out of the rec room toward his office, his phone buzzed with a voicemail. When he tapped the screen to listen to it, though, there was only silence on the other end. Hmm. He deleted the message and continued on.

EMBER DIDN'T EVEN see the strike coming, but she certainly felt it, like a Mack truck slamming into her at full speed. White hot pain exploded in her face. Then she was free-falling for several excrutiatingly long seconds. She landed flat on her back, her head cracking against the hardwood floor. Everything went dark.

Agony woke her, blazing through her right jaw and cheek. Tears flooded her eyes and rolled down her temples into her hair. She was afraid to move, in fear that the pain would escalate. Her stomach roiled with nausea.

Somebody clutched her hand, squeezing and shaking her. She wanted to tell them to hold still, because they were hurting her more, but she couldn't get her brain to shift into gear. Hazy sounds reached her ears, but it was like they were packed with cotton. Muffled.

Taking a deep breath, she forced her eyes to open. After much fluttering and tearing from the brightness of the light overhead, she was able to focus. Her father knelt beside her, her hand cradled in his as he tried to wake her. His eyes were anguished as he realized she'd woken and was staring at him. He raised her hand and pressed a kiss to the back, but she pulled it away.

He'd done it again.

She lifted a hand to her jaw, and wasn't surprised to find it grossly swollen. It throbbed with pain, and she wondered if he had broken it. Taking a fortifying breath, she opened her mouth a tiny bit.

Fire burned down through the side of her face, neck and chest. It was all she could do not to cry out again. There was a very real possibility he had broken her jaw. She took a moment to catalog the rest of her body, but the only injury appeared to be her head. Laying here, she could feel a knot forming on the back of her skull.

Possible concussion. She wouldn't know until she got checked out.

Using her hands, she pushed up from the floor. Dizziness made her sway on her bottom, but she breathed deeply, dragging in oxygen to stabilize. She felt his hand on her back, but it would have taken more effort to shrug it away. She just didn't have it right then.

She glanced at the hallway, but everything seemed to be quiet. It still looked dark outside, so she probably had a few hours before Drew woke up looking for her. How the hell was she going to explain this to him?

She blinked, realizing she'd sat there for several minutes. She was losing time, definitely a bad sign. She needed to get up.

Easier thought than done.

Eventually she rolled to her hands and knees, but couldn't formulate what to do next. When he reached down to help her, she let him, but pulled away to sag against the hallway wall. Listing to the left, she staggered down to the bathroom and flicked on the light.

Fresh pain seared her head, and a few tears escaped her control to roll down her cheeks. Even *that* hurt.

She forced her eyes open.

God, it was bad.

Her jaw was blazing red and swollen. Purple bruising had already started to spread out from the strike, and she knew she would be ten different colors in a couple of days. It had already started to darken below her eye. There were a couple of deeper purple lines in the main bruise, from his individual fingers. How the hell were they going to explain this away?

He stood in the dark hallway, arms crossed, eyes haunted as he watched her.

Ember opened her mouth to speak, but it was too painful. He saved her the trouble.

"I'll stay here with Drew while you go to the hospital."

She nodded and lowered herself to the commode while he called her a taxi.

ZEKE SCANNED THE bar when he walked in, but didn't see Ember right away. When he'd gotten up the courage to go in to pick up their order on Tuesday, a day he knew she normally worked, she hadn't been there. He'd asked for her, and the hostess's gaze had slid away, as if she had something to hide, then said something about family time. The words sounded forced to him.

He'd waited three days. As he and Chad waded through the crowd now, he felt a little ridiculous checking on a woman who'd spoken less than fifty words to him. Zeke couldn't yet articulate what he felt for her, other than a huge need to know more about her.

Chad seemed to understand what propelled him. He went to Frog Dog with him, because he admitted to being curious where she'd gone as well. Literally, Ember had never *not* been there when they'd gone in. She owned the place with her dad. It wasn't like they could just pack up and leave.

A different young woman waited on them. Chad poured on the Texas charm, blue eyes twinkling, grinning even as the waitress surveyed the scars winding down his neck. "Is Ember working?"

The girl blinked and smiled, obviously remembering her job. "She's in the kitchen. Do you need her?"

"Yes, we do. Can you get her for us?"

Zeke swallowed as the girl disappeared, anxiety tightening his chest. He didn't know what he would say to her, if anything. His damn brain stalled out at the most inopportune times. He just needed to check on her for his own peace of mind. Her father had been having issues when they'd last talked to her.

The waitress returned with their beers in hand and an apologetic smile. "Sorry guys, she says she's cooking and really busy right now. Can she talk to you another time?"

Zeke's internal alarm went off and the tension in his gut increased. The grill wasn't especially crowded, and he doubted there were that many food orders. Pushing to his feet, he met Chad's eyes and circled the waitress. "B-back in a…minute."

Without hesitation, he went to the swinging kitchen door and pushed through.

Ember looked up when he walked in, and when he saw her face, he felt like he'd been gut shot. Heavy bruising discolored the right side up to her eye, and she seemed to be in pain. Her mouth was pinched and her eyes squinted. When she realized he wasn't one of the wait staff, she immediately turned away.

"No customers allowed back here," she called. She

moved down the cook line and motioned to a Hispanic man she was working with to take her place at the grill. Zeke prowled down the parallel aisle until he was right behind her.

"L-look at me."

She shook her head stubbornly. "You can't be back here, Zeke."

"Look at me, please."

After a long pause, she turned her body toward him, but kept her face turned away. Bending his knees enough to peer into her eyes, he waited until she looked at him.

Fury rolled through him as he realized he could see finger marks within the bruise. "Who d-did this to you?"

She shook her head and refused to answer. Tears glinted in her eyes. "It's no big deal, okay? Accidents happen. I was just in the wrong place at the right time. It happens when you own a bar."

Her eyes slid away and he thought there was something she wasn't telling him, but he had a feeling if he called her on it she'd clam up completely. He reached out to touch a length of her dark hair that had escaped from her braid.

Her eyes flickered and a single tear rolled down her cheek.

He groaned. "D-d-don't cry. I didn't come in here to …up-upset you. Just had to check on you."

EMBER DIDN'T KNOW why his halting words disarmed

her when nobody else's concern had, but they did. Another tear escaped. Then another. She swiped them away, but they just seemed to fall faster. The events of the past week weighed on her, and she had decisions to make that were going to change their lives even more. For just a heartbeat in time, she wanted to *not* be strong.

When the big Marine pressed a gentle kiss to the top of her head, she leaned into him and curled her hands beneath her chin, desperate for some kind of anchor in the catastrophe her life had become.

His massive arms wrapped around her and she broke into sobs, unable to tamp them down any longer. She heard rumbling beneath her good cheek, but couldn't understand the words. When he swung her up into his arms, she didn't even care, as long as he continued to hold her. She heard the squeak as her office door slammed shut, then the world tilted as he sank onto the old couch pushed against the wall.

Time stopped as she sobbed into his shirt and he gently rubbed her back. He was so solid and strong beneath her fists. It felt like the world could be falling down around them and he would still hold her safely above everything. A warrior battling back the nightmares.

She lost track of time as she cuddled into him, but her tears eventually began to dwindle away. Embarrassment rolled in as she realized how soaked his T-shirt was. She ran her hand over his broad chest. "I'm sorry, Zeke."

His grip tightened around her as she tried to pull

away. "It's okay. J-just a shirt."

Ember let him hold her for just a minute more before her pride forced her to sit up on his lap. She started to slide off, but he grabbed her hands in his. "What can I do to help?"

She blinked, unused to even being offered help. It had been her and her dad for so long, then Drew had been added to their little group, and they were pretty self-sufficient. That had all changed now, though.

She shook her head as she realized she was going to have to ask for help. "I don't know. I have to move, and find somebody to watch my son. But I have to be here, too, to make sure everything runs right."

When she lifted her gaze, his bright blue eyes were solid and reassuring. She choked out a laugh. "I can't believe how much I'm trusting you right now. I hardly know you."

He grinned at her, and the scar that looped down from his bottom lip pulled his smile off-kilter. "I'm a Marine. I'm a...good guy. Even though I don't look it."

Against her better judgment, she grinned too, then flinched when it hurt her jaw. "Ouch."

His eyes drifted down her face and he raised one hand as if to touch her, but stopped. "Who did this? Really?"

She looked down at her lap, debating what she could tell him. Everybody would probably know eventually anyway. "My dad. I walked into our house last Saturday and it was dark. I thought he was sleeping, so I just started to walk through the house like I always do, but he was having a flashback."

He tensed even further beneath her and his cool blue eyes darkened with anger. "PTSD?"

She nodded. "Although he doesn't think so. He just has 'dreams' he says."

"Where is...h-h-he now?"

"In jail. I pressed charges against him, hoping that he would finally get the help he needed. The week before Christmas." Fresh tears rolled down her cheeks, but he wiped them away with gentle fingers. "I think he understands, though, because he hasn't bonded out, even though he has the means."

Zeke nodded and tapped his chest, over his heart.

"He knows? Maybe. I love my dad so much, but he could have seriously injured me. As it is, he gave me a concussion. And this." She waved at the marks on her face. "If he'd done this to my son, he would never have seen me again. Us."

Zeke tipped his head in agreement, and Ember appreciated that he wasn't trying to stand up for him, in some misguided Marine solidarity. She already felt like shit for putting her father in jail; she didn't need somebody disagreeing with her actions.

"All...veterans n-need counseling. Sometimes the older ones m-more. Because th-they didn't get it when they came home." He smiled his lop-sided smile. "You're...lucky he didn't break your jaw. No fun, beli-lieve me."

He sounded like he spoke from experience. Her eyes traced across his beard. She curled her fingers into her palm to keep from running them over his square jaw.

"You did fine," he continued. "I w-would have done the s-same thing."

Zeke wasn't anybody to her, just a guy that came in sometimes that she had a bit of a crush on. But she appreciated hearing those words, more than he would ever know. She took a deep breath, relieved that she'd finally told somebody. She slid off his lap. "Thank you. I know you've got better things to do than coddle me, but I appreciate it."

He stood up in front of her, and Ember was struck with just how massive he really was. Double her size, at least, with an arm span for miles. His black T-shirt stretched across his chest but billowed around his narrow waist. She'd felt the strength of his body, and it was truly something. No wonder those frat boys hadn't messed with him.

He held his hand up to tuck her hair behind her ear, and she was fascinated by the sight of his bicep knotting, and the shirt cuff straining. She couldn't get both hands around that arm, let alone one.

"I don't mind," he said softly.

When he looked at her that way, the expectations of the world kind of fell away, and she found herself leaning into his touch. When she realized what she had done, she jerked back.

Oh, hell no.

"I'm sorry I cried on you," she said briskly. She didn't have time in her seriously effed-up life for a man.

Again, he gave her that reassuring smile. "A-any

time."

Somehow Ember knew he meant it, and it scared her. Her eyes traced over his harsh face, with his mottled skin. He shifted at first, then made himself stand still under her scrutiny. Pink started to suffuse parts of his face. "Do they hurt?"

He quirked his mouth and shook his head. "Not much."

Ember wondered at the flat tone. He must be in pain but didn't want to admit it. "Mind if I ask what happened?"

Zeke sighed and crossed his arms over his substantial chest, letting his hair fall over his brow. "Afghanistan. Grenade hit c-c-corner of a building I was taking c-cover behind, and a c-c-cinder block wall came do-down on me. Ripped me up good. Smashed my head. Gave me a TBI. Broke some…bones. Jaw."

"What's a TBI?"

"T-traumatic brain inju-jury."

Ember cringed in sympathy. "Damn. How long ago was that?"

"Three years."

So, still fairly fresh. She wondered if he had dreams about the war like her dad did. When she asked, he quirked his mouth again.

"Sometimes. I don't…punch people though."

Ember looked away, feeling like an idiot. How long had she lived with Dad's eccentricities and thought they were just that? Just part of her dad.

When her mom died years ago from cancer, they'd

both been left reeling. The sickness had come on so suddenly, and no matter how aggressively they attacked it with round after round of chemo and radiation, it hadn't helped. Almost a year exactly from the date of diagnosis, she'd been gone.

Dad had had a heart-attack the same month Mom died. Ember had still been in college then, but she'd dropped out when he got sick. It was while he'd been recovering that he punched her the first time. She'd gone in to check on him early one morning, and had gotten slammed in the kidney as she leaned over him to adjust the blanket. He'd been disoriented at the time, and they'd both chalked it up to a fever, but her back had ached for a solid two weeks. He'd apologized and they'd moved on.

Dad had recovered, but it'd been a slow process. Almost more than she could manage on her own. After the better part of a year, he was almost back to normal. When she mentioned going back to school to finish her business degree, he'd supported her, and seemed to be making a new life for himself. He bought the restaurant and moved closer to her at school.

When she'd found out she was pregnant several months later, the situation wasn't ideal, but she'd been overjoyed. And her dad had been as well. The father of the baby hadn't been. He'd dropped out of school and disappeared. It had seemed natural to move in with her father to let him help with the baby. It was when she was walking the halls with a colicky Drew that she realized her dad had more serious issues. He would wake at odd times, pore over a scrap book from the war, and sometimes snap at her more aggressively than the situation warranted. It had been startling and frightening, and she wondered why she'd never noticed his behavior before. Had Mom known? Surely.

She blinked, realizing that Zeke stood watching her, brows raised. She felt her skin flush and shook her head. "Sorry. Wool gathering."

The facts were starting to add up, and she hated feeling stupid. She should have noticed it a long time ago.

"Have you f-found a place to move?"

Ember hesitated, struck with a feeling like she stood at a crossroads. If she told him she had chosen a new place, she would be committing to be more engaged with him. She would be admitting she needed help, which just rubbed her self-sufficient streak the wrong way.

He honestly seemed like a nice guy. Earnest. She hadn't gotten any asshole vibes off of him yet.

She could just blow him off and say no.

Glancing around the cluttered office, and thinking about the work she had to do at home, she realized that she had so much on her plate that she would appreciate a little help.

"Maybe. Any chance you have a truck?"

He grinned, and she caught her breath at the emotion shining in his stunning eyes. "I do. A big one."

Ember's brain made the immediate jump to the inappropriate and she felt color suffuse her face. She'd been so aware of him for so long. Zeke dropped his gaze to his boots. He appeared to be just as embarrassed, although he had a wide grin on his face. She kind of got the feeling that he hadn't talked like this for a while. His looks would probably discourage a lot of women, but they appealed to her. He looked comfortable to her, like a favorite sweatshirt that had been through many softening washes.

Probably not what he wanted to hear.

"I can't believe how uncomfortable this makes me, asking you if you can help me move. I'll pay you back for gas and food."

He shook his head, grimacing. "I ..." He shut his eyes, obviously searching for a word as he waved a hand. "Offered. I work n-nights, but my d-days are free. I can help anytime."

Coughing into his hand, he reached into his back pocket for a worn billfold stuffed with post-it notes. He dug for a minute and pulled out a black and gold business card. "That has my ce-cell number on it."

Ember took the card with a glance. Zeke Foster, investigator, Lost and Found Investigative Service.

"I found an apartment complex not too far from here online that sounds good," she told him. "I'm going to look at it tomorrow. If it suits us, I'll put a deposit down." She frowned. "Are you sure you want to help me move? If something comes up you're definitely not obligated."

He shook his head again, gaze solid. "N-nothing will come up. I'll help you. M-may bring a buddy or two for f-f-furniture."

Ember sighed and slipped the card into her back pocket. "Okay, Zeke. Thank you."

He looked like he wanted to say something else, but he shook his head, gave her a crooked smile and left the office. Ember stepped out enough to watch him walk away. His broad, T-shirted back filled the doorway as he pushed through the swinging door into the front and disappeared.

Her tummy quivered with spent emotion, and her face throbbed. All the crying hadn't helped her ever-present headache. She stepped back inside the room and pulled a bottled water from the mini-fridge on the floor, then shook some ibuprofen into her hand. Gulping them down, she settled into the office chair behind her desk.

Zeke had been incredibly sweet, carrying her away from the kitchen and prying eyes to care for her. She'd have struggled through everything if he hadn't come in, but she couldn't deny that she felt better after crying it all out. Just telling somebody what was going on eased her worries. She had no idea if what she was doing was right, but she had to do what her gut told her to do. Dad needed help, but he wasn't going to admit it easily.

Watching Zeke struggle with the stutter made her heart ache. The fact that he'd been injured in the war was suddenly very real to her. Military guys came in all the time, but she'd never gotten close to any of them. Certainly not close enough to worry about their safety when they left.

I'm glad he made it back okay.

It made her wonder what her dad had been through.

CHAPTER THREE

THE APARTMENT SHE found suited her needs perfectly. On the ground floor, so she didn't have to worry about carrying boxes, and eventually groceries, upstairs. There were two bedrooms, two baths, a nice sized living room and a decent kitchen. It wasn't very old, so the appliances and carpet were fairly new. They could move in immediately because it was vacant. But the best thing was that there was a single mother one building down who watched children. The manager told her about Ms. Miller when she mentioned she needed somebody dependable. As soon as she knocked on the woman's door and saw the happy kids inside, she knew Drew would be fine. The preschool would deliver him here, and Ms. Miller would watch him until Ember got home. So much better than the overcrowded daycare she used now.

It wasn't ideal, but damn close. They would have to make it work.

The manager of the complex looked at her with pity in her eyes and not a small amount of wariness. Ember knew she looked bad, and the makeup she'd painfully tried to apply didn't even cover a portion of the Technicolor bruise. She'd left her hair hang over her shoulders today, in hopes that she could kind of shield her face.

Drew was not thrilled with the move. Her father had watched him for four years, ever since he was a baby, and he didn't understand why Grandpa wasn't there now. It was impossible to explain to a child that sometimes lives had to change, and sometimes those changes were hard. And that people had to go through bad things before they could find the good. So, she settled for telling him that Grandpa was sick and he was getting help, but that they wouldn't be able to see him for a while. He pouted but nodded that he wanted Grandpa to get better.

His mood improved when she showed him the playground, just on the other side of the building. As he played on the wooden fort, she called Zeke.

"Lo?"

The sound of his raspy baritone sent chills up her spine. He had no business sounding so delicious.

"Hi, Zeke. Did I wake you?"

She glanced at the clock on her phone and winced. One o'clock. He'd said he worked night shift, so she probably had.

"Nope, I'm wide awake," he spoke through a yawn.

She chuckled, appreciating the fib. "Well, I'll make this quick. I checked out the apartment and I've put a deposit down. Were you serious about helping me? Even though it's supposed to be snowing the next couple of days?"

"Of c-course. G-give me your address and what time

you w-w-want us to be there."

Ember gave him her dad's address, trying not to get choked up. Today was visitation day at the jail, but she hadn't wanted to see him until she had moved out. She'd heard from the prosecutor that the domestic violence charge was going to be suspended if he completed an outpatient counseling program.

That had probably gone over like a ton of bricks with her dad, the original Mr. Stubborn.

"How old is y-your son?"

Zeke's question brought her back to the conversation. "Four. He's kind of lost right now. We've lived with my dad all his life. He doesn't know anything else. So this is going to be a challenge. Especially with Christmas right around the corner."

"Mm, I th-think he'll be fine. Kids are...are...are...well, they bounce back okay."

She heard the frustration in his voice at not being able to articulate what he meant, and she had to bite her lips to keep from supplying the word. Somehow she knew he wouldn't appreciate her speaking for him.

"Yes, I know he will." She sighed. "As a single parent, though, I can't help but want a secure life for my son. This year he's had a lot of changes, because he started preschool too."

"Ah." He kind of laughed over the line. "Bu-but was it ha-harder for you than him?"

Ember blinked and sat back. For the first time realizing that missing her son during the day, when they normally played, *had* brought her down. "You know, I didn't realize it until you said it, but I think I have been taking it harder than he has. He's meeting new friends and getting to see things. But I've kind of been moping without him. I do feel guilty because I'm working when he gets out of school, and he has to go to daycare now."

"I don't kn-know what your po-po-position is at the bar, but you may think about trying to change things there. Do what Chad said, and manage."

Ember realized she could change some things. Dad used to work during the day, then he would head home in the afternoon to relieve her. Why couldn't she do the same thing? One of the assistant managers immediately came to mind who could be her alternate. Deena always asked for more responsibility. Options started tumbling around her brain.

"Thanks, Zeke. I don't know why I didn't think of that, especially now."

"T-too close to the problem."

"I guess so. Well," she sighed, "I should let you get back to sleep. We've both got big days tomorrow, and I need to get packing."

"Okay, Ember. I'll see you tomorrow."

"Night, Zeke."

She pulled the phone away but hesitated to hit the disconnect button. The line clicked and the screen went blank without her doing anything, so she stuffed it into her pocket. Thoughts of Zeke lying in bed, sheet tangled around his hips, teased her. Even while she'd been crying in his arms, she'd been very aware of the power wrapped around her. Nobody had ever held her like that before.

She wanted to feel it again.

ZEKE CLOSED HIS eyes, replaying every word of their conversation in his mind. Ember's sweet voice tickled against his insides, making him wish for more. Whether she realized it or not, she had hooked him good.

He'd gotten used to sly whispers about his looks. He couldn't say it didn't still hurt sometimes, but after a couple of years he'd built up some armor. Ember was the first woman to look at him like he wasn't a freak. Like he was still a man who could be depended upon. And he had to admit, it felt good coming to her rescue. She needed help, and they were going to help her.

After they got her moved, he'd just have to play it by ear. Maybe he'd get up the gumption to actually ask her out.

The thought made him smile as he drifted back to sleep.

EMBER PUT HER management plan into action immediately. She called Deena at home and asked her about covering her shifts for a few days, until she resolved some personal issues. Deena jumped at the chance, promising that everything would run smoothly. Ember made her pledge that if anything came up, she was to call.

If anything happened to Frog Dog while her dad was

gone, her ass would be grass.

Deena's enthusiasm and calm-headedness reassured Ember immediately. She promised to call in and talk to the young business major at the close of shift.

Then Ember went to work. Mrs. Miller was happy to take Drew, so she had some kid-free time to get things in order. Maybe she could get a head-start on the next day.

For the first hour she packed she cried. She had moved five years ago, when she found out she was pregnant—her son had grown up here—and she'd left her mark on it. From the rugs on the floors to the colors on the walls, she had tried to make the house as much of a home as she could for Drew. And for her father. She'd seen the loneliness in his eyes after Mom died, and Ember had tried to ease his sorrow, in little small ways like her mother had.

She wrapped and packed for hours. Till the tips of her fingers were sore from running across newsprint so much. Her back ached from hauling boxes and she had a headache from banging pans together.

At three o'clock she went and retrieved Drew. He blinked his big brown eyes at her and curled into her arms as she carried him to the car, tired from playing all day. Ember's throat tightened with love as she buckled him in, pressing a kiss to his dark hair. He was worth whatever she needed to do to keep him safe.

When she finally allowed herself to fall into bed later on that night, she groaned with exhaustion, slipping away almost immediately.

IT TOOK EMBER a long minute to realize the doorbell was ringing. She sat up in bed and looked to the right for her alarm clock. But it wasn't there. She lurched out of bed and grabbed her cell phone off the dresser. Eight forty-eight.

Shit!

That had to be Zeke at the door.

Shit, shit, shit!!!

She hadn't taken Drew to preschool. Wait, it was Sunday.

Her life was so seriously going to hell in a hand-basket.

She shoved her arms and legs into the only things she could find, the dirty sweatshirt and jeans from the night before. Her bra was nowhere to be found, and she didn't have time to look for it.

The doorbell rang for a second time.

Bolting out of the bedroom, she arrived just in time to hear Drew ask Zeke, "What happened to your face?"

Her own face burning in humiliation at her son's rude question, she pulled Drew around to face her. "You need to apologize to Zeke. That was not nice at all."

Zeke chuckled and knelt down beside them. "It's okay. I much prefer the actual cu-curiosity of a child."

He looked the boy in the eye. "Hi Drew. I'm Zeke. My face got hu-hurt when I was a Marine and trying to help some people. Did your mom ever tell you the Humpty D-d-dumpty story?" he waited for the child to nod. "Well, I'm kind of like Humpty, only the wall fell on me, and broke me."

Drew's dark eyes widened dramatically, and he looked at Zeke with new respect. "Really?"

The big man nodded. "It did. Then they c-couldn't put me back together j-j-just right."

Her son cocked his head to the side as he did when he was really mulling something over. Then he reached out a little finger and traced one of the scars on Zeke's cheek and down through his beard. "Does it hurt?"

Again that shuttered look crossed the big man's expression. "No, it doesn't hurt. Not now."

Curiosity satisfied, Drew turned to her, wrapping his arms around her neck. Ember ran her fingers up his sides and lifted him high. "We slept in today, didn't we?"

He shook his head, dark eyes shining with humor. "You slept in."

"Yes," she sighed. "I did. Can you be a super good boy for Mommy today? We're going to start moving boxes over to the new apartment."

He started to nod, but frowned when she mentioned the new place. "What if Santa can't find me when I move?"

"Uh, well, I think he'll know."

He blinked at her. "I already sent out my letter, though. He thinks I live here."

"He-he's got G-g-PS."

Drew looked at Zeke. "What?"

The big man waved a hand. "Oh, yeah. He's got GPS. He follows the signal from your mom's phone."

Drew frowned, looking between the two of them. She nodded and tried to look like Zeke knew what he was talking about. Eventually, a broad smile spread her little man's mouth. "Okay."

He wiggled to be let down. As soon as his feet touched the carpet, he was gone. Ember could hear cartoons on in the living room.

She smiled up at Zeke. "Thank you. You kind of saved my bacon there. I didn't know what to say."

He winked at her. "When I was his age the mo-mo-most...mo-most..." Waving his hand in frustration, he grimaced and stopped to take a deep breath.

Color suffused his cheeks, and her heart ached for him. But she waited patiently.

"It's sp-special," he finished. "S-sorry."

"Don't be sorry about anything. Please. It doesn't bother me." She tried to reassure him with a smile, but he just frowned all the harder and shoved his hands into his jeans pockets.

"B-bothers m-me." He shook his head, obviously exasperated, and looked away from her. Hair fell over his eyes, and he didn't bother to brush it away.

She dared to reach out and touch his elbow. The muscles of his arm were clenched tight and his massive hands were fisted in his pockets. "I don't know anything about your injuries," she said softly, "but it sounds like it gets worse when you get frustrated, right?"

He didn't have to say anything. She knew.

"Well, there's no judgment here." She stepped back to give him breathing room. "Coffee?"

With a tight nod he followed her to the kitchen.

Drew had made himself at home in the kitchen while she'd been sleeping. Cereal was strewn everywhere, and a chair was pushed up to the open door of the fridge. She couldn't help but laugh as she put the jug of milk away and replaced the chair at the table. "That's what I get for sleeping in."

She glanced at him enough to see the glint of a smile, then started assembling the coffee.

"I have just about everything packed I'm going to take. I think." She leaned her butt back against the counter top. "A week ago I never would have imagined I'd be in this position."

"You're doing the right thing, though. S-sounds like your father n-n-needs help."

Ember kept telling herself that, but it didn't make it any easier.

"Unfortunately," he continued, "the court may file a restraining order between you. Has your...l-l-" he waved a hand, "said?"

"My lawyer? No, he hasn't."

The thought of not being able to see her father at all made her sick to her stomach. It would kill him not to see his grandson. For the millionth time she prayed she was doing the right thing.

Zeke leaned down to look in her eyes. "You are."

Was she that transparent, that he could see everything on her face? The turmoil she was going through wasn't normal for her. She'd had a charmed life up to now. Yes, there'd been sorrow and challenges, but she had still had a clear direction of travel. Make the business flourish, raise her child to be a man better than his own father. Now she floundered. She didn't know what to do about her dad, and she was worried about the future of the business they shared.

Utmost in her mind was protecting her son. Part of that was by moving out of her father's house. Period.

Zeke was still smiling at her in reassurance and she took a deep breath to stabilize. But it backfired. His subtle, spicy scent flowed into her and she had to draw in a deeper breath. Something dangerous unfurled in her belly and she couldn't help but respond. Her unbound breasts peaked to attention and her eyes latched onto his mouth. Unable to help herself, she reached up with the tip of a finger and touched the line that slid down through his full lips, tracing it down his bearded chin. He jerked back from her, scowling.

Ember winced at the guarded look she'd put in his eyes and dropped her hand to her side. "I'm sorry, Zeke. I didn't mean to crowd you."

He gave a short laugh. "It's j-just been a while since anybody's touched me like that," he admitted softly.

Ember swallowed, feeling awareness spike between them. She dared to lean forward, just a bit. "So, how long has it been since somebody kissed you?"

Desolation swept his rough features and he dropped his head, but not before she'd seen the vulnerability. And the flash of anger. Muscles twitched in his square jaw. Ember felt like an ass. The question had to have sounded incredibly insensitive. "I'm sorry…"

He chopped her off with a hand in the air. "Don't worry about it."

Spinning on his heel, he left the kitchen, leaving her aching and feeling guilty. The coffeemaker let out a final gasp and she jumped. Damn it.

All the way down the hallway, she cussed under her breath. Then again when she went to the bathroom to brush her teeth and hair. She wouldn't have kissed her either looking the way she did. The bruise spread across her jaw and up toward her ear, although most of the swelling had gone down. There was some shading beneath her eye, but it hadn't been enough to give her an actual shiner. She knew it would be at least another week before she looked normal again.

She heard masculine voices out front and rushed to get ready, scraping her hair into a ponytail. Wondering how she could get rid of that desolate look on his face.

ZEKE SHOOK CHAD'S hand. "Th-thanks for helping o-out."

Chad made a face at him, blue eyes twinkling. "Did I have a choice? I don't remember hearin' that part. You told me to clean out my truck and be here because the little waitress was in trouble. You're lucky I know the boss and was able to get time off."

Laughing, Zeke pounded his buddy on the shoulder. He counted Chad as one of his best friends, and he knew he'd do a lot more than help him move a woman. Hell, the last two reconstructive surgeries Zeke had gone through, Chad's had been the face he'd woken up to.

When Ember walked into the room Chad's eyes widened with surprise, then narrowed with anger. "Damn. Zeke said you'd been hit, but he didn't say how bad."

Ember brushed her cheek with her hand. "Yeah. It doesn't really hurt anymore."

Zeke knew better than that. He'd seen her wince twice this morning already.

"Thank you so much for helping me. If I had a truck I'd do it myself."

"No problem at all. I think there may be one or two more coming." Chad waved his scarred left hand. "Can't do any heavy lifting with this thing, and although he thinks he could probably carry a couch on his own, ole Tiny here will probably need some help."

Ember laughed at the nickname. "Do they really call you Tiny?"

Zeke shook his head. "Only when they n-n-need their asses k-kicked." He punched his friend lightly in the shoulder and the other man staggered.

"Get off me, you clown, before I shove a cowboy boot up your ass." Chad wiggled his leg to show off new boots.

"Oh, m-man. Those are nice." Zeke was happy for his buddy, because he'd been waiting for them for months.

Chad grinned, all Texas pride, too smug for his own good. "I know."

Their interaction set the tone for the rest of the day.

Brian Claypool, one of the more recent hires, arrived with Ortiz. They didn't have trucks, but they did have an SUV, and the balance and muscle needed to help move the big items.

Ember ran around like a mad woman, in stark contrast to the military precision the men brought to the situation. Chad was the obvious one in charge, even ordering Ember through a controlled list of objectives. Within an hour, they had the first load of furniture ready to transport.

She called for the boy to get ready to go outside, and he came running. His enthusiasm dimmed when he found out they were going over to the other apartment. "Can I ride with Zeke?" he asked.

Zeke blinked in surprise, curious why the kid wanted to even be near him. Drew smiled up at him with clear-eyed trust, and he couldn't help but give him a wink.

"Well, I don't know, honey." Ember's big brown eyes looked up at him, and he knew she wouldn't crowd him if he didn't want her near.

"You c-can ride with me."

He regretted the offer almost immediately, but Drew whooped for joy. He jabbered excitedly when he caught sight of the Zeke-sized black truck. Ember transferred Drew's booster chair from her car to the back seat of his vehicle, shoving a couple of boxes to the side.

Chad grinned at him when he noticed Ember shuffling, and Zeke felt his face heat with embarrassment. Shoving his sunglasses on to keep out the glare of the snowy day, he shook his head.

Excitement ran through him, too. Interaction with people outside his direct group of coworkers was minimal. Interaction with women-almost zero. His speech therapist didn't count. At the office he did background searches and record checks for the most part, with the occasional overnight stakeout thrown in for variety, and reported to Chad and Duncan. He had very little contact with the outside world.

Which suited him fine. His brain had been scrambled and he couldn't be depended upon for more important tasks until he'd unscrambled it. But after three years, his progress was slow. He had a feeling he was as good as he was ever going to get.

As he started the truck, he glanced at Ember. Even with the bruise discoloring her face she was beautiful. She had a black winter coat pulled up around her chin, and tan ear muffs over her ears. She smiled at her son as they pulled out of the driveway.

"You'll have your own room just like before, and this spring we'll decorate it for you."

The boy didn't say anything so she turned forward to give Zeke directions to the new apartment. He could tell that her son's non-response hurt her feelings.

"I have a feeling you'll f-find kids your age to p-p-play with. You said they have a playground?"

Ember nodded. He glanced at Drew in the rearview mirror. "That would be nice, right?"

The little boy scrunched up his face. "I guess."

He didn't seem hopeful, though.

"And I can already tell you like it at Ms. Miller's, right? It sounds l-like she had several little kids your age."

Drew didn't respond.

Zeke sighed. It had been a long time since he'd had to deal with his nieces and nephews, so his rusty conversational skills were deserting him. Not to mention, he was hyperaware of the woman sitting beside him, her vanilla scent curling around him. The slightest move she made he felt. She'd dressed in an oh, so provocative Broncos sweatshirt with cupped her full breasts perfectly, and her jeans looked like they'd been spray painted on her. Watching her bend over to pack items and move boxes had been torture, and kept him agitated all day.

Flurries started to fly as they pulled into the apartment complex Ember had chosen, so they all started to move a little faster. The apartment building itself looked well-kept and safe, so he felt better about moving her into it. Ember stood in the doorway of her new apartment and directed the men where to place things. Within just a few minutes the once empty space was substantially fuller.

Brian talked to Drew as they walked down the hall-way, asking him where he wanted his bed when it was put together. Zeke carried Ember's headboard into the opposite bedroom and started to put together the frame. Even just handling her bed had him semi-aroused. It didn't help when Ember came in carrying a box for the closet. She dropped it to the floor and arched her back, swinging her arms above her head. Her full breasts pressed against the material of her sweatshirt, and the bare skin of her stomach peeked out. She was unaware he sat just a few feet away from her.

Tightening the last bolt into the frame with his Leatherman, he deliberately made noise. She glanced at him and smiled, then seemed to catch herself. "Sorry, it's a little strange having a man in my bedroom."

Zeke was unable to tear his gaze away from the pink tinge coloring her cheeks. Her straight hair was in another ponytail, disheveled yet sexy at the same time. He wanted to toss the elastic, just to see what she looked like with her hair down. Beautiful, of course, but he wanted to see it for himself.

Another want he could add to his ever expanding, never-gonna-happen list.

He pushed to his feet to stand in front of her. "I'm nobody."

EMBER STARED AFTER Zeke's retreating back. Why would he say that? He wasn't really that down on himself, was he?

They finished unpacking the larger items, then she locked up with her brand new key and they loaded into the vehicles to go back to her dad's house. Drew fell asleep in the back seat, little action figure clutched in his hand.

"I think one more load and we should be done," she

told Zeke, just to break the silence of the truck.

He glanced at her. "Are you sure? S-seems like there's still a l-lot of stuff there."

"I know, but I can't take everything. I'm only taking what I know I've bought. Eventually Dad will get out of jail and come home." She rubbed a hand across her forehead. "I feel guilty enough taking what I have. It's going to break his heart when he discovers we've moved out."

"You can't keep worrying about that," he told her firmly. "If one of the-the waitresses came in, bl-black and blue, what would you have told her to do?"

"Move out. And not to hesitate."

Zeke nodded, waving a big hand as if to say 'there you have it'.

In her mind, she knew she had taken the correct path. It was just hard telling her heart that.

She ordered several pizzas to be delivered for lunch as they finished loading the trucks. The snow had tapered off and a weak Colorado sun was shining. While the guys ate, Ember wandered through the house, looking for things she'd forgotten. She ended at her father's den, reluctant to enter. There probably wasn't anything of hers inside, but she was going to check.

When she opened the door, the smell of her father's favorite leather chair rolled over her, and her heart clenched. She wished for a time when everything had been good. When Mom had been cooking in the kitchen and their shared laughter had filled the air.

Dad's worn scrapbook lay on the floor. Crossing the

room, she retrieved the leather-bound tome and sank into the chair. A tumbler of his favorite Kentucky Bourbon sat on the end table, as if he'd just gotten up to close the blinds or tuck his grandson into bed. She flipped the book open to the page it had been spread to.

It was a news article, dated from March first, nineteen sixty-eight. *'The Marines have prevailed at the Battle of Huế…at the cost of 5000 civilian lives'.* She recognized her father's old Company name, and knew that he had been in Vietnam at that time. Her eyes drifted over the words of what had to be her father's history.

Zeke came in a few minutes later with a stack of pizza for her and a cola. Ember stared at the plate in his hand, honestly surprised he'd thought of her. "Thank you."

He set the cola beside the glass of bourbon. "If I'm bo-bothering you I can go."

She shook her head, looking back down at the news article. "Do you know anything about this battle? My father has never said anything about it. But there are several derogatory articles about it in here, and I recognize my father's company name."

Zeke knelt on the floor beside the chair and she turned the book to him. He read for a few minutes, then glanced up at her self-consciously. "I didn't get through the who-ole article, but I recognize the name. Huế, pronounced *way*, was a major cl-clash be-tween the North Vietcong and the Marines and South Vietnam. The N-north snatched power and held the city for a month. The Marines couldn't get a break and were…outnumbered. But they f-f-fought on, and recaptured the city. B-but, most of it was gone. Like eighty p-percent of it. That was when support from home started to change."

"Really?" She'd never have known any of this, but was willing to take his word for it.

He nodded, tilting his chin so that she didn't see as much of his face. She'd noticed throughout the day that he would shift to keep the more damaged left side out of view.

Wish he wouldn't do that.

Those marks were badges of courage. Nothing else.

"They couldn't get h-heavy…heavy artillery into the town, so they were l-l-l-l-literally under weapon fire every day. And they had an agreement with the g-g-government not to bomb anything. So they couldn't get air support."

She flipped through a few pages of news articles, then came upon a page with an envelope stapled to it. There was something lumpy inside it. Curiosity got the better of her and she flipped it over, leaving it attached to the page. The envelope itself was open, so she slid her fingers inside the flap and fished out the item.

A Purple Heart. Even she knew the significance of the medal.

Zeke whistled through his teeth and reached out a finger to brush against the enamel. "They didn't give these out very often b-back then, and a lot of times it was y-y-years after they'd returned home."

Why hadn't Dad said something about this? She had

known he'd been in the Marines but he'd never whispered a word about receiving the Purple Heart. Mom hadn't mentioned it either. She flipped through the book and found another envelope, this one a small manila with 'Frog Dog' scrawled across the front. There were several more uniform ribbons and awards inside. She shook her head. "Why wouldn't he be proud of these?"

Zeke shrugged and his ice-blue eyes darkened. "S-sometimes you fall into…s-situations where you have no choice but to fight. A lot of guys don't c-co-consider that being courageous."

Her throat tightened with emotion and she blinked hard. "It must have been one of these buddies that died."

He seemed to think the same thing, because he didn't disagree. Carefully and reverently, he repackaged the ribbons and medals.

Ember appreciated his care. It made her proud that her dad's service could inspire that kind of respect.

"Was your family in the military?"

Blinking, he shook his head. "There may have been sh-short stints, but for the most p-p-p-part my family are farmers. They own a…d-dairy in Ohio."

She laughed and couldn't help but reach out to squeeze his bulging deltoid muscle. *Oh, yeah.* "So that's how you got so strong. You grew up drinking your milk like a good little boy."

His eyes flared with heat and he glanced away. "S-s-something like that."

Pushing to his feet, he set the book on her father's

desk, then turned to the shelves lining the far wall. Her father had a massive collection of books, on what seemed like every different subject. As she ate her pizza, she watched Zeke go from shelf to shelf, looking at the spines. He stopped to look at a book, and Ember caught her breath. Just the way he stood, with the light hitting his dirty blond hair, feet planted, faded blue T-shirt straining around his massive bicep, made her want to cross the room and snug herself up against his gorgeous ass. She'd wrap her arms around his waist and cuddle in.

Reaching for the cola, she took a couple of huge swallows. The guy was helping her out, but all she could do was ogle him. Each of the others were cute too, in their own way and in spite of their injuries, but Zeke tugged at her heart.

"Has he read all these?" he asked.

Ember set her plate aside and stepped up beside him in front of the paperbacks shelf. "These, yes, some many times over. My dad always has a book close at hand. There's a stack behind the bar at Frog Dog of loaners. His buddies come in here and there and they swap books. I guess it's the masculine version of a book club."

He glanced at her and smiled.

"If you see something you'd like to read, I'm sure he wouldn't mind. Just leave it at the bar when you're done."

Zeke winced and reached out to run his finger over the spine of a recent bestseller. "I used to-to read a lot, but after the e-e-explosion I can't... untangle words like I used to. Takes a long time."

"That must be so frustrating. Do you listen to books on tape?"

His blue eyes twinkled as he looked down at her. "I do. Es-specially when I'm on surveillance."

She grinned at the enjoyment in his rough face, but he must have gotten uncomfortable with the attention, because he turned away.

Ember pursed her lips in aggravation. Being injured the way he was, she wondered if he would even try to pursue an attraction. Maybe it was up to her to forge through his protective walls, so to speak.

Zeke drifted over to her father's guitar in the corner of the office. He stared at it for a few long moments, before glancing at her over his shoulder. "Mind?"

She shook her head, curious what he would do with the old acoustic. It had seen better days and Dad kept it more for sentimental reasons than practical. Zeke picked it up and dust swirled away. He fitted it under his arm, running through chords to check to see if it was in tune. It wasn't off by much, but his broad fingers tweaked and tightened until it was at perfect pitch. Seamlessly, he strummed the opening chords to "Home" by Michael Buble.

Ember knew her mouth had to be hanging open, but she didn't care. As if he couldn't *not*, his deep voice fell into accompaniment. She stepped away to sink down into a chair, entranced by the broken man singing, eyes shut. Tendrils of need and longing crept into her heart, and it was one of the most beautiful things she'd ever seen. Tears filled her eyes.

Almost halfway through the song, his fingers fumbled a note and he stopped singing. When she lifted her eyes to look at him, he stared at her as if he'd forgotten she were there. Jaw tight, emotion brimming in his eyes, he set the guitar back on the stand and walked out of the room.

Ember could have wept. She didn't know why he'd quit, but she wanted him to come right back in and finish the song. Her mind knew what melody was supposed to come next, but it couldn't create the same type of emotion he had while singing.

She thought back to the absolute absorption on his face as he sang, and realized he hadn't stuttered or hesitated once through the entire performance.

CHAPTER FOUR

FTER CLEANING UP the pizza mess, she locked the house for the last time. As she jogged down the steps and sidewalk to Zeke's truck, her throat tightened at the thought of not being able to plant flowers this year. Drew's swing set was still in the backyard. Their lives for the past several years had been right here. Perhaps once all this mess had blown over she'd be able to bring him home for a visit.

She would call her lawyer tomorrow and let him know they had moved out, and that her father could post bond. If there was a protection order in place, they'd have to work opposite shifts at the restaurant. It would be a pain in the ass, but it could be done. If not, though, she'd have to think about finding other work to support herself and her son. Or, she'd petition the court to remove the protection order.

Leaving the restaurant didn't scare her as much as she thought it might. She had a business degree under her belt and several years' experience helping her father. She had enough of a cushion in the bank to carry her through for a few months if she was frugal.

In her heart, though, she didn't want to leave Frog Dog Grill or her dad.

She didn't say anything to Zeke about the guitar, though she couldn't help replaying it over and over in her head.

The men unloaded boxes like they were professionals, separating them room by room and putting them as out of the way as possible. The apartment was packed by the time they were done, but it would be manageable.

Bryan and Diego cut out early. She offered them gas money, but they refused, as she'd suspected. Ember hoped it was a couple days before they noticed the money she'd stuffed into the ashtray.

Zeke and Chad hung out and started helping her unpack boxes. Toward evening, she ordered Chinese takeout and they took another break. Chad connected the TV and Drew fell asleep in front of it almost immediately, oblivious to the movement around him.

They ate from paper plates in the living room, sitting on the couch and chair.

"I can't thank you guys enough," Ember admitted. "I can't believe we got everything moved today."

Chad grinned at her as he slurped up a noodle. "Well, you had a squad of Marines at your disposal, but you're on your own, now. My leg is killing me. I'm gonna have to roll out."

Scooping another forkful, he wound them around the tines, then shoved the mass in his mouth. After that final bite, he shoved the plate away, hand on his lean stomach. "I shouldn't have eaten all that." Even as he said it, though, he snatched up a fortune cookie to stuff in his pocket.

Ember walked him to the door and gave him a quick hug. "Thank you for helping. I know Zeke talked you into it but I really could not have done it alone."

Blue eyes crinkling, he tipped his chin to her. "No, problem, Ember. Maybe I'll see you next Saturday?"

She nodded. "I'll be there. And the first round is on me."

He grinned. "I might take you up on that."

When she returned to the living room, Zeke had started to gather up the leftovers.

"I can get it."

He shrugged those broad shoulders and continued to clean up. She moved to help him.

Zeke seemed to be walking a little stiffly, but she didn't want to be nosy to ask him why. They put the leftover Chinese in the fridge, though she knew it would probably be gross the next day. She threw the trash in the can and leaned back against the counter.

"What was wrong with Chad's leg?"

Zeke glanced at her, dark blond brows lowered. "The new pr-rosthetic must have been rubbing. He doesn't usually say anything about his p-pain."

Ember blinked and realized her mouth was hanging open. "Wait, he's missing a leg? Are you serious?"

He nodded. "His left. That's why he was sh-showing me his b-b-boots earlier today. He just had them...f-fitted for the prosthetic."

She thought he'd just been showing off his cowboy boots. *Dipshit*. She thought of all the boxes he had carried and all the trips he had made for smaller things.

He'd never mentioned anything of the sort, and she'd not even noticed a hitch in his gait. "Damn, I feel even worse that he helped me now."

Zeke frowned at her. "Why? Just b-because he's missing a leg it doesn't mean he's any less of a man. He doesn't want to be kn-known by his injuries. None of us do."

Ember snapped her mouth shut, chastened. "You're right. I'm sorry."

He smiled a half-smile. "Chad will ap-p-preciate that you didn't even notice. He's self-conscious enough about the arm."

"It looks painful," she said. She led the way back to the couch and sank down into the corner.

"If it is he doesn't say." He sank down on the opposite end and leaned forward to rest his elbows on his knees. He scrubbed his hands over his face.

"Are your scars painful at all?" She held her breath as she waited for his answer.

He glanced at her out of the corner of his eye. "Not so much. Th-this one," he traced his finger over the deepest one across his forehead and down through his eyebrow, "has been the worst. My skull was cracked and my occ-occ-c-ciptal bone fractured. I have a couple of sc-screws holding it together. I get headaches here f-f-fairly often."

"And there's nothing the doctors can do for that?"

"Well," he looked away, "they can m-make it look better but they can't do anything about the h-h-headaches. I think I'll always have them. I have...m-medication if they get really bad, but I can only take it if I know I'm not going to be doing anything for the next twelve hours."

Ember crossed her arms to keep from reaching out and wrapping them around him. "How long were you in the hospital?"

He quirked his mouth as he thought. "Months. I had no b-balance when they first got me up, and I couldn't string ten words together. It took a long time to re-re-l-learn all that stuff."

"Was your family there with you?"

He shrugged. "Some. Mostly at first. I finally sent them home because they were j-j-just sitting there. Not doing anybody any good." He looked at her fully. "Do you n-not have any family around here?"

She shook her head. "No, my dad has a brother out west somewhere but they haven't talked for a long time. Not sure why. I have several cousins I talk to once a year. My mom was an only child. It's always just been my dad and I. Then later Drew came along." She smiled as she looked at him stretched out on the floor, pillow beneath his head.

"And what-what about his dad?"

"Well," she sighed, "he didn't want to be bothered with a kid. He was just getting through college. He signed over all his rights and I've never heard from him again."

Zeke leaned back into the couch as he looked at her son on the floor. "He helped m-make him. He should have stepped up."

Ember appreciated the sentiment, but she was just as responsible. "We were both really young, and didn't plan on doing anything in the first place. It just kind of happened. Thinking back, though, I wouldn't have changed a thing. It gave me my son, so how could I?"

Quiet descended between them and she felt her eyes getting tired.

"Well, I should go."

Pushing to his feet, Zeke waded through the boxes to the front door. Ember followed along behind, reluctant for him to leave. The silence had been easy and comfortable.

He paused by the door long enough to pull his heavy canvas coat on.

"Thank you, Zeke. For everything."

Ember stepped in front of him and wrapped him in a hug. His heavy arms came around her head, carefully cocooning her. She felt him press a kiss to the top of her head, but it wasn't what she wanted. She pulled back enough to stare up into his eyes. His squeezed shut and he turned his head away, trying to let her go.

"Would you kiss me, Zeke?"

He exhaled harshly. "Not a g-g-good idea, Ember."

"Why? Do you have a girlfriend I don't know about?"

"You know I don't," he snapped.

She pulled back, alarmed at his response. "No, I don't know that. You're a good looking guy—" she got no further as he ripped out of her arms and jerked the door open. "Hey, wait a minute!"

She grabbed his jacket before he stepped through the doorway and jumped in front of him, blocking his way. Fury darkened his blue eyes to navy, surprising her with its intensity. "Why are you pissed? Because I said you were good looking?"

He snarled and shook his head. "Are you fucking blind? Or just cruel? Because either way I'm d-done. I need to go."

Her mouth dropped open, furious that he could be so incredibly wrong. "Now wait a minute. You've been with me all day. I'm not blind and I'm definitely not cruel. You know that. I actually do think you're good-looking. Hell, you're built like a damn underwear model and have the prettiest ice-blue eyes I've ever seen. Yes, you have scars, but they certainly don't bother me, or turn me off. If anything, they turn me on, because they tell me exactly the kind of man you are." She poked his hard chest for good measure and stepped into his space. "Now, are you going to kiss me, or not?"

"No." He looked out the door, over her head, his eyes jumping.

"Why not?"

His jaw clamped shut.

"Why not, damn it?"

He shook his head, mute, and his shoulders slumped, as if he couldn't hold out any more.

"Because if I do I'll never be able to stop."

His gaze landed on hers and for the first time, Ember started to reconsider her approach. There was a vulnerability in his expression that made her question whether she was woman enough to fulfill his needs. But the attraction she felt for him was beyond anything she'd ever experienced before. She took a breath.

"Maybe I won't want you to stop."

She'd barely gotten the words out before his mouth crushed hers, forcing her head back. But it didn't matter, because Zeke's mouth was finally *on* hers, moving back and forth as if they'd talked about the moves beforehand. Ember staggered under the desperate wave of need that hit her. Her legs went to jelly and her heart raced as she poured her own enthusiasm into the kiss.

Zeke growled deep in his throat and wrapped his arms around her again, this time to pick her up and swing her around to brace against the foyer wall. She felt him shift down below and heard the door slam shut, then his hips were aligning with hers. She jerked as she felt the ridge of his erection nestle in against her pubic bone and without thought she wrapped her legs around his hips. Immediately, his hands shifted to grip her ass.

Zeke froze against her, then pulled his mouth away from hers to kiss first her bruised cheek, then down her neck. "I don't know if we should do this," he whispered. But his hands clutched her ass, and he flexed against her again.

"You're right, we shouldn't," she gasped as she arched into him.

Groaning, his lips found hers again, as if he couldn't stay away. Ember shuddered as his tongue swept into the depths of her mouth. The aggression in the move startled her, but also spiked her arousal. His heavy chest crushed her breasts, but the feel of him against her, panting for breath the way she was, exhilarated her.

One of his broad hands slid up her side, beneath her T-shirt, to the swell of her breast. Sliding his thumb between their bodies, he pushed beneath her bra to stroke over her hard nipple. Ember cried out, tearing her mouth away. "Oh, yes. Please, Zeke."

Shoving her bra out of the way, he gripped her whole breast in his massive hand, plumping and smoothing. Her womb clenched in need as he savored her body. Then, with a final nibble at her lips, he pulled away.

"I don't have anything to protect you with, Ember. I have to stop."

His hand pulled away from her breast, and the other palm holding her ass began to lower her to the floor. Ember could have wept in denial. The muscles of his arms trembled, and she knew it had to be costing him as well.

For one wild moment she thought about throwing caution to the wind and letting him know that she had a five-year IUD in, but pulling away would probably be prudent. Her life was in turmoil and she didn't know if she could be part of a relationship right now, in spite of the monumental need she had for him.

Her feet settled to the floor and her knees almost gave out. She clutched at his arms, unwilling to let him go. He stroked her hair, seeming just as reluctant.

"M-maybe w-w-we could g-g-o out someti-time."

Ember smiled at the obvious nervousness in his deep voice and nodded her head against his chest. "I would love that."

Finally, he pushed away from the wall and straightened, looking down at her. His were still dark, hard with determination and his jaw was clenched, as if the battle not to take her waged on inside him. Her eyes flickered at the thought and fell to the obvious erection behind the zipper of his jeans. She moaned and one hand lifted as if to touch him, but he jerked away.

"Don't."

His harsh face had reddened in parts and paled in others. He blinked and took another step back. Ember crossed her arms beneath her breasts, cold without his warmth. "Call me," she whispered.

With a single tight nod, he turned and let himself out of the apartment.

Ember shivered and sank down against the wall as the cold air swirled around her.

AROUSAL RODE HIM hard, and it was all he could do to get to the truck and inside. He cranked the ignition, then just sat there, dragging oxygen into his lungs. Flashes of brutal memory assaulted him and he tightened his hands on the steering wheel, afraid that he would run back to bust right through her door and take her standing up. She'd cradled his face in his hands as if the marks didn't matter, and that acceptance was heady.

But it was a treacherous road to walk.

He didn't know if he could trust his own gut because

it had been so long since he'd been involved with anybody. She'd seemed genuine in her need, but maybe he was just a body, scratching an itch.

The thought of her breaking down at the restaurant flashed across his mind and he had to rethink that assessment.

Shaking his head, he shifted into gear, glad that he'd taken the night off. It would give him a chance to get her out of his system.

CHAPTER FIVE

THE CELLPHONE BUZZED on the desk beside him. Duncan looked at the screen and recognized the number from the other night when they'd all been working out. The caller had not left a message, just a hangup. This was the same number.

Sliding his finger across the touchscreen, he rocked back in his chair.

"Hello."

Somebody was on the other end of the line, he could sense it, but they weren't saying anything. "Can I help you?"

The line disconnected.

Duncan rolled his chair until he could look out the window to the street below. Snow-covered, of course, but no worse than normal for Denver three days before Christmas. He followed the line of sidewalk down as far as he could see, but nothing caught his attention.

He hadn't seen Aiden for several weeks now. Now that he knew who the hunched figure was, he always watched for him. If the other man needed help, Duncan wanted to be there to give it.

Pushing to his feet, he wandered toward Palmer's office. The other man was behind his cluttered desk, staring off into space. When Duncan walked into the office, he visibly started.

"You okay, there, buddy?"

John swiped a hand over his face and grimaced. "I'm fine. Just thinkin'. What do you need?"

Duncan showed him the cell phone number and John's fingers flew over his keyboard. "This number has called me a couple of times, but doesn't say anything. I just want to see if I can figure out who it is."

John sat back in his chair with a shake of his head. "Nope. The number looks like a drugstore throwaway. Dead end."

He thought as much, but it was good to have it confirmed.

"Is the holiday covered? The Malone surveillance and…"

John nodded, but he didn't look happy about it. "Harper volunteered to work the entire weekend, with Claypool pulling day shift. Parks is still on the Vail detail, with Calvert backing him up. We have a secondary contractor taking over for Roger while the plant is shut down so he can fly home for a couple of days. Everything is covered."

"Did you find something for Shannon?"

John's face darkened with a scowl.

"Fuck, Duncan, do you know how hard it is to shop for a damn woman? I've never had to deal with this before, so I'm seriously struggling. I don't know what the hell she wants. Besides a damn ring, I mean."

Smiling, Duncan shifted a pile of manuals from the

only chair in the room.

"Have you talked to her at all? There has to be something she wants."

John sighed. "She wants to get married, I can see it in her eyes, but I don't know if I'm up for that yet. Hell, I just moved into her house. I'm getting used to the cats. I don't know if I can do any more than that right now."

Duncan felt for his buddy. He'd probably be freaked if he were in the same situation.

"Well, why don't you think about getting away for a while. Take a trip or something. Shannon would probably love to get out of the house for a while after the Gerbowski mess."

John blinked and cocked his head to the side. "You know, that's not a bad idea. Even if I have to travel."

Duncan left his second in command surfing travel sites and planning a trip.

He limped his way down to the rec room and raided the refrigerator, pulling out some easy to eat essentials. Twice before, he'd left a bag of food where Aiden had hung out, and twice before they were gone the next day. That wasn't to say that somebody else hadn't taken them, but he didn't think so. The industrial park where the office building was located did not have any homeless.

Other than Aiden.

As he climbed into his truck a few minutes later, Duncan had little hope that he'd see the other man. But as he pulled out of the parking lot, he kept his eyes peeled.

When he pulled up to the spot where he'd seen Aiden before, he stepped out with the bag in his hand. Planting his cane, he carefully walked to the dumpster where he'd been curled up before.

And stopped dead.

Blood soaked the snow-covered ground in a wide circle, exactly where Aiden had sat that first night. Duncan scanned his surroundings, looking for a body, but he didn't see any suspicious lumps. And there was no trail of blood leaving the area.

What the fuck?

There was no sign of anything on the ground beneath his feet, so he backtracked to his truck to leave the crime scene pristine. Then he called Denver PD.

The young officer that arrived hadn't been on the job long, if the way she paled at the sight of the blood pool was any indication. She quickly called for her supervisor, then the supervisor called for a lab tech and the detective on call. Duncan answered the same questions over and over again, but he didn't have a great deal of information. He gave them Aiden's name, but hell, he didn't even know if that was his real name.

The detective that came, Roberts, didn't seem concerned that a homeless person was missing and presumed injured. Didn't even seem to care that it was a veteran.

"Even more reason to off himself then," he shrugged.

Duncan had never been more livid. "Listen, Officer," he deliberately left off "Detective", and leaned into his space, "I don't know what your problem is, but if you need to ask somebody else in that will treat this with the respect it deserves, I'll wait." He crossed his arms over his chest as the snow swirled around them and waited as Roberts blustered through a series of threats. Duncan held up a hand. "I have Quillen's number. Do I need to call him instead?"

Using the Captain's name had been a gamble, but it shut the man up, and sent him scurrying back to the scene. Duncan waited outside as long as he could, but the cold was making his bones ache. He slid inside the truck to stay warm.

When the lab tech started to pack up his stuff, Duncan stepped out to ask the man a single question, and he didn't like the answer he received. Yes, from the volume of blood available on scene, it would be enough of a loss to kill an average sized man. The tech couldn't presume if it had been an attempted suicide or assault, though he did confirm that there were no obvious signs of struggle.

Duncan climbed into his truck and headed for home, heartsick.

EMBER TIGHTENED HER grip on her purse as she walked up the steps Monday afternoon into the courthouse. Her lawyer, Quinn Roberts, stood just inside, and he grimaced when he saw her.

"Thank you for coming down so quickly, Ember. When I told the judge's secretary you had moved out, she thought your dad would be a good option for early release, especially since you want to remove the PO. Because of the weather and the holiday, the jails are jam-packed right now, and they need the room."

He paused long enough to look her face up and down.

"I had hoped that the bruising would have faded by now. When the judge sees that he could reverse his decision and leave the protection order in effect."

Ember winced. "I could try to go cover it up more, but it becomes more obvious that I'm hiding something after a certain point."

He nodded reluctantly and took her elbow to guide her down a long hallway. At one of the many doors, he paused and let them inside. A woman with a plastic smile greeted them, and ushered them directly into the judge's office. The balding man behind the desk barely glanced up from the folder of papers in front of him.

"Have a seat, please. I'm just reading over the motion." He looked up at Quinn. "Your client is aware of the danger of removing the PO, correct?"

"She is, Your Honor."

Shrewd eyes peered at her over the tops of his glasses and the judge frowned. "Was your jaw broken, Ms. Norton?"

"No, sir."

"But you did receive a concussion, right?"

She gave a tight nod.

"So, why should I remove this order? Mr. Norton hurt you, and badly, I must say."

"I know, Your Honor, but I believe he suffers from

untreated PTSD. After a week of mourning the loss of his friend, I spooked him in the middle of the night. He lashed out. I just happened to be there. I do not believe it was anything personal."

The judge tapped his pen on the desktop and stared at her for a long moment. "I've talked to your father and I would agree. I am hereby lifting the order, effective immediately. Mr. Norton does have to complete a forty week outpatient PTSD program. Have no further violations for five years. He owns a restaurant with a bar. Has he ever had a drinking problem?"

Ember shook her head. "No, never. He hardly drinks, actually."

"Make sure he doesn't. That will be all."

Quinn hustled her out of the judge's office and back out to the main foyer. "That went better than I expected."

Nodding, she stepped against the wall so that other people could get by her. "So, Dad can get out of jail now and get back to his life, right?"

Quinn nodded. "The charge has basically been dropped as long as he completes the counseling. If he falters, he'll have to go back and face the criminal charges. Just don't let him falter."

She shook her head. "I won't. Thank you."

She walked down the street to the county jail and left money for her father's account. She wasn't sure exactly when he would be released, but at least he'd have money for a cab when he did get out.

Ember walked back to her car and slid behind the

wheel, exhausted from worrying about everything. Surely her dad must feel even worse. When he got home there would be no one to meet him, no one to talk to. No little boy hugs.

Her eyes welled with tears and she dashed them away. He would be out within a few hours, and they could go from there.

She glanced at her cell phone, tempted to dial a number she'd only called once before yet had still memorized. It had been almost eighteen hours, and Zeke hadn't called. Maybe he didn't feel the same way she did.

Damn. Was she really counting hours now?

ZEKE LOOKED DOWN at the cell phone in his hand and debated calling Ember. To see how she'd settled into the apartment. To see how Drew liked his room. To wish her almost Merry Christmas. To see if she still needed him as much as he needed her. He'd had daydreams from hell all night, taunting him with things that would never be.

His phone buzzed, scaring the shit out of him. Ember's name appeared on the screen.

Dad's getting out today.

Panic clutched at his gut. *So,* he typed, *is that good?*

Yes, I think so. We'll see.

Fury erupted in his chest and he almost smashed the

phone against the dash. The guy that had damn near broken her jaw and left her marked was going to be near her again. And she was going to let him. Adrenaline poured through his system and it was all he could do not to leap out of the truck and find some poor schmuck to pound on in the street.

In the corner of his brain, the tiny, little rational part started to make itself known. He took a deep, rib-expanding breath and battled back the negative emotion. Grabbing the pen and post-it pad from the dash cubby, he scrawled a note to remind himself of the incident next time he spoke with the counselor.

Then the worry for her safety invaded. When he needed to be worrying about his own issues.

Let me know when you meet with him, so that I can check on you afterwards.

Ok. I will.

He kept refreshing the fading screen, hoping another message would pop up. But she must have left to do something else.

Starting the truck, he pulled out of the parking lot. Glancing at the seat beside him, he called himself ten different kinds of fool. When he'd unpacked a few boxes in the living room, he'd discovered Ember's love for elephants. The little figurine he'd bought wasn't expensive, but it was cute, with the baby elephant sitting splay-legged, as if he'd been knocked down. He'd also gotten Drew a Spider-Man action figure, but he worried that it would be a little old for him.

Foolishness. He hadn't called her, so he had no plans to see her, and Christmas was just a couple days away. She wouldn't want to spend it with him anyway. She had her son, and now her dad. By the time he did see her, the holiday would be past, and he'd feel like a damn fool if he gave her the gifts then.

He smacked his hand against the steering wheel, frustrated. He didn't know what he wanted from Ember right now. Heat surged through his body, as if to give lie to his thoughts.

Checking the side view mirror, he slid into the left lane to get ready for a turn. He'd toyed with the idea of whether or not to try to catch a flight back to Ohio, then discarded it almost as soon as it formed. There was no way he could. The Agency was officially closed Christmas Eve and Christmas, though their running cases were covered. He had to work directly before and after. His mom and dad were disappointed, but they understood. Some of the guys were meeting at John and Shannon's house Christmas Day, just to hang out and be social. He hadn't decided if he would go yet, but he was leaning toward it.

Shannon had done wonders for John's disposition. Last year at this time, when Zeke had first started, John Palmer had scared the shit out of him. The former Gunnery Sergeant had been the epitome of the perfect Marine, loud and dominant, upright in all things. The wheelchair hadn't seemed to have changed his basic disposition at all, and Zeke looked up to him for his spirit. He was the Marine Zeke had wanted to be, and didn't get the chance to be.

Since John had gotten involved with Shannon, though, he'd changed. A little more approachable, a little more accepting. Definitely more laid back. Shannon, on the other hand, a woman who had always been kind and sweet, was even more so now. Nothing ever riled her.

Probably because she knew she had a lethal guard dog at her side.

He would love to have a chance at what John and Shannon had. But he didn't know if he had the courage to reach for it.

Glancing at the gifts on the seat beside him, he promised himself he would stop by Ember's apartment on the way to work.

EMBER PACED THE apartment. Dad was supposed to be over in less than twenty minutes for dinner, and she had no idea what she was going to say to him. They needed to talk, desperately; it would just be difficult to break the initial ice. As she circled the couch, she flipped a couple of box lids closed and snapped on a floor lamp. Then repositioned the new couch pillows. And picked up a couple of stray Legos. Nervousness ate at her, and she hated feeling like she needed to be on guard with her dad. She headed to the kitchen to check the casserole in the oven, then sent Zeke the text she'd promised him, telling him her dad would be over.

When Dad did eventually knock on the door, she had to take a deep breath before she swung it open.

Her first thought was that he looked older, worn, as if the week in jail had aged him many years. Guilt overwhelmed her, because her father was not a young man.

"Now, stop it," he growled. "I can already tell we're both going to be battling the guilt, so let's get the apologies out of the way. I'm sorry about that night. I just wasn't thinking clearly. I'd been remembering things and for a minute, the past blended with the present. I'm so very sorry. I would never hurt you for the world." His dark eyes filled with tears as he cupped her bruised cheek. "You were right to file that charge against me, because it got me thinking. I probably do have some of that post-traumatic, shell-shock stuff, so I'll go to the counseling. I promise. And I'll be able to have your trust again if you decide to leave Drew with me."

A tear slipped down his cheek, and it broke her heart. She lunged into her father's arms, crying. "I'm sorry I had to do that, and I'm sorry I had to move out of the house. Drew has to be my first priority, though."

She could feel him nodding against her in agreement. For a long minute, they just stood there in the doorway, with the cold swirling inside, and held each other.

Her father pressed a kiss against her head. "I know, honey. And you did exactly as I expected you to do. I knew we couldn't live together for a while. So I didn't bother posting bond. It gave you a chance to get out and get settled, and it looks like you did a wonderful job."

She pulled back and glanced around. There were still many boxes to be emptied.

"I had help, actually."

As she ushered him inside, she told him about the Marines that had come to her rescue and helped her out in a pinch. Her father seemed leery, then fascinated as she told him about the group from the bar. His eyes creased with humor and she realized she'd mentioned Zeke a few times. She shrugged. "It feels like he could be important to me. I've never reacted to a man like this."

Her father looked intrigued. "Sounds like a big deal."

She laughed, because Zeke was definitely a force of his own. "He definitely is."

Drew came tearing out of his room just then and smashed into his grandfather, wrapping his arms around his waist. "Where've you been? I missed you and missed you. And missed you some more but you never came. Do you feel better now?"

"I know, Buddy, but I was kind of tied up with some things," he shot a smiling look at her as he hoisted the boy in his arms. "And yes, I feel better."

That look told her that her father was fine with the events the way they had unfolded. His sense of humor had served him well over the years, and it would now as well. The huge knot of tension in her stomach began to ease.

They had a wonderful evening. Ember explained the few shift changes she'd made at the restaurant and Drew talked about his new sitter and the friend he'd made. Although the surroundings were now different, the night itself was amazingly the same as many others they'd had together. Dad tucked Drew into bed as he had for the past four years.

She was surprised when a knock sounded on her door. Even more surprised when she found Zeke standing on the step. She sucked in a breath at the harsh beauty of his face shadowed by the overhead light. "Hi." She smiled, ridiculously happy to see him. She swung the door wide in invitation. "Come in, please."

He glanced inside for a moment, then shook his head. "Nah, I j-just wanted to ch-ch-check on you, make sure you were okay after seeing your father. And bring you these." He held out two wrapped presents.

Ember blinked at them, surprised even more that he'd brought them gifts. One was wrapped in a child's paper, and the other in a striped silver foil. They were both beautiful. "Zeke, thank you so much. You didn't have to do this."

He shrugged uncomfortably and glanced over his shoulder, as if thinking about escape.

"Can you come in?" she asked.

He started to shake his head, but his gaze narrowed in on something over her shoulder. His face hardened and he straightened to his full height. "I can come in for a few minutes."

Ember stepped back and let him through. Determination rolled off of him as he walked straight to her father standing a few feet into the living room. Ember quickly shut the door and followed.

Zeke towered over the older man, and his jaw had

hardened. He dropped his coat to the chair as if to show off his powerful, heavily veined arms. For a moment Ember thought he would do something rash. But instead, he stopped inches away and put his face uncomfortably close to the other man's. "I appreciate the sacrifices you made for your men and our country, but if you ever lay a hand on Ember again, accident or otherwise, I think I'll have to teach you some manners."

Rather than back away, her father leaned toward Zeke, with fire in his dark eyes. "I don't know who the hell you think you are, but you need to get out of my face."

Zeke stayed exactly where he was, and her father suddenly snapped. He slammed his hands into Zeke's chest, trying to get him to back off. The move hardly budged the bigger man, though, which seemed to infuriate her father even more. He took a swing at Zeke, catching him square in the jaw, just like he'd done to her.

Ember cried out, fearing that her father would be hurt. Or have another heart attack. She'd never seen him so angry.

He took another swing at Zeke. Rather than take it like he did before, Zeke caught the older man's fist in his hand and just held it. "I want you to look at the way you are acting."

Her father struggled to free his hand, swinging with the other, but Zeke had no problem holding on. "Mr. Norton, stop. You're overreacting."

The anger took a solid minute to fade from her father's face. Blinking several times, he eased his body back.

Zeke let go of his fist. "I wanted you to see how little it takes to trigger an outburst. Until you start to get counseling for your issues, you could be a danger to Ember and Drew."

She caught the shine of tears in her dad's eyes before he spun away.

Ember felt terrible, but she too was shocked at how little it took to send him off. She looked at Zeke. He regarded her carefully, as if waiting for her to rip into him. She forced out a small smile and shook her head.

When her father turned around, he'd gained control of his emotions but still seemed rattled. He rallied, though, and nodded to Zeke. "I appreciate you demonstrating that. I didn't even..." his voice faded away.

Ember stepped forward when he looked at her, and it broke her heart to see how defeated he looked. She stepped close and wrapped her arms around him. He tried to pull away, but she didn't let him. "I love you, Dad. I know you'd never deliberately hurt us."

He wrapped his arms around her and held her close. "Obviously, though, I have no control over my emotions right now. He's right."

"The shock of your friend t-t-taking his own life is enough to...s-s-s-stir all this up."

Ember appreciated the kindness in Zeke's voice. He could have been a shit, rubbing it into her dad's face that he was so out of balance, but he didn't.

"And it would b-be n-n-natural to want to follow your friend."

Ember couldn't contain a sob against her father's chest.

"But those f-feelings pass. We've all had them, and c-c-continue to have them when things get rough. But it can't be an o-out. You're a Marine. You're better than that."

She felt her father nod against her head, and pulled back to look up at him. "You damn well better not take your own life. You have too much to live for."

Sighing, he cupped her bruised cheek. "I know, Ember. It's not an option for me. Never has been."

A black cloud that had been following her around for the past several weeks drifted away with his words. She'd just needed that small reassurance from him.

The two men apparently came to some masculine understanding, because Zeke shoved out his hand. Her father clasped it strongly and shook. "Hank Norton."

"Zeke Foster."

When they stepped out of the handshake, Ember took a shuddering breath. For a minute she'd thought Zeke was going to pile drive her not-insubstantial father into the ground.

A shiver coursed through her as she took him in. Big and aggressive and beautiful. But it occurred to her then that he'd never been a threat to her father. He wouldn't use his size and power against somebody like that.

Tears came to her eyes as she looked at his red cheek, where her father had struck him. Zeke had taken that hit to prove a point to her dad.

"Zeke, can I get you some ice or something for that?"

He scrunched up his face and waved a hand.

"Can I get you some dinner? We ate a little bit ago, but there's plenty more."

She crossed the room to put the presents under the little artificial tree she'd set up, then headed for the kitchen. Rather than wait for an answer, she dished out some of the chicken casserole, put in it the microwave for a minute and grabbed a pop and a spoon. She ran her hands through her loose hair and bit her lips, wishing she'd put some makeup on. Too late now. The microwave dinged and she carried the items out.

Zeke stood where she'd left him, arms crossed, but her father had pulled his coat on. She looked at him in dismay, but he waved her concern away. "I'm going to go home and enjoy my bed for the first time in a week. Thank you for dinner, honey."

She handed the plate of food and pop to Zeke. Hugging her father, she tilted her cheek up for his normal kiss and walked him to the door. "If you're sure, Dad."

"I am. I'll call you tomorrow. If you're comfortable running the grill I may take some time away."

Ember nodded. "Of course. Take all the time you need."

"Okay." He cupped her bruised cheek again, and with a sad smile walked out into the snowy night.

Closing the door after her dad, Ember took a relieved breath. As she turned to look at Zeke, he winced at the look on her face and set the food on the end table.

"I know it pr-probably ap-appeared harsh, but I had to s-show him."

She sighed as she walked across the room to stand in

front of him. He shifted as if he were going to move away, but she didn't let him. Fisting her hand into his T-shirt, she pulled him down close enough that she could cup his scarred face and press a kiss to his red cheek.

Zeke seemed shocked that she would touch him, because he didn't respond for a heart-stopping moment. Then he relaxed into her, cradling her head in his hand and angling his mouth to cover hers.

Ember's nipples tingled as if he'd touched them, but he hadn't. It was just remembered, banked need from the night before. Arousal rolled through her lower body.

If he hadn't wrapped his arm around her back, she'd have fallen. The man made her weak in the knees. And head. She needed to catch her breath before she did something rash.

Damn it, he tasted too good.

She dragged her mouth away and pushed her hands against his shoulders. He released his hold immediately, making her stagger. He turned to face the dark window so she couldn't see his expression.

She reached out a hand to touch his back but he leaned away from her.

"It's okay," he growled. "Re-really. I get it. I just read too much in to-to-to the si-sit-...yeah, fuck! I should go."

"Zeke, wait."

But he had already turned toward the door, snatching his coat from the end of the couch. Ember rushed to intercept him, afraid that he'd leave before she had a chance to explain. "Stop, damn it."

"I don't need your p-pity, Ember."

She jumped in front of him just before he pulled the door open.

"What the hell are you talking about? The kiss?"

He grimaced, lending a darker edge to his face. Anger flashed in his look. "Yes, the damn kiss. A simple th-th-thank you would have b-been just fine. You didn't have to act as if y-you wanted m-me."

She frowned. "I wasn't acting. I do want you."

He snorted, shaking his head. "It doesn't matter."

"It does. I just haven't been in this position before."

"What po-position would that be, Ember? Being attracted to somebody who's so fugly he disgusts you? And can't fucking talk? But feeling obligated to try to pay him back for standing up for you with your father?"

"Quit saying that, damn it! You have no idea what I'm thinking. Yes, I am attracted to you, but the only thing fugly about you is your attitude right now." She shoved her hair away from her face, angry, then held up a single finger. "I've been with one man in my life. One. And I had a son from that one night. So excuse me if I would like to try to slow down and enjoy this." She waved a hand between them.

Zeke blinked at her as if he didn't believe her words. "One man?"

She pursed her lips and crossed her arms over her breasts, unwilling to repeat herself.

"You didn't pull away because of my scars?"

Ember shook her head at his bullheadedness. "No, I didn't pull away because of your scars. Believe it or not, I like your scars. And your stutter doesn't bother me." Unable to help herself, she reached up and ran her finger over the faded silver line that ran into his lip. "But I won't just sleep with somebody again because it's convenient. I need more out of a relationship than that. And while I do appreciate your help with my dad and everything, I'm offended at the insinuation that I'd sleep with you to pay you back."

Zeke winced and leaned back against the wall beside the door. He tipped his head back and barked out a laugh, Adam's apple bobbing in his strong throat. When he looked at her again, his eyes were more calm. "I'm sorry I s-said t-that. I was just being de-de-defensive, I guess."

Ember could understand the reaction, but it was hard to hear. "Zeke, I wouldn't have you in my home right now if I didn't feel something for you. I felt something the first time you walked into the grill."

She could feel red creep into her cheeks, but she maintained the eye contact, knowing it was important to him.

"I d-d-did too."

A warm feeling curled though Ember's belly at his quiet admission, tempting her all over again. "Really?"

Reaching out, he tugged on a section of her hair. "I wanted to see this down around your face. Or spread across a pillow."

Ember shut her eyes as the vision hit her.

"Or swaying as I rock you from behind."

She moaned and something released in her lower

body. She shifted, wet panties dragging against her sensitive skin. Her nipples had already hardened, chafing against her clothes. She itched to rip her sweatshirt and bra off and cash in on his words. It had been so long since she'd felt like this. No, she'd never felt like this.

When she opened her eyes, Zeke's face had suffused with color and he stared at her hard, obviously waiting for some kind of indication of what she wanted. One hand flexed against his side. As she watched, his second palm reached forward to cup her breast.

Ember didn't wait for his hand to connect. She leaned into his touch, gasping as his thumb immediately started to stroke back and forth over her nipple. "Oh, God. More."

Zeke grasped a handful of her hair in his hand and tilted her head back for his kiss. Ember cried out as his mouth settled on hers and his other hand left her breast to cup her pelvic bone, grinding the seam of her jeans into her heat. She arched her hips into his touch, desperate for more. As his tongue swept inside her mouth, he tightened his fist in her hair, forcing her to accept every bit of him.

Sensation overwhelmed her as his touch tried to burrow through the fabric of her jeans and inside her. His strong hand forced her up onto her tiptoes as he moved unrelenting fingers back and forth over her pelvic bone, and her clit.

Ember whimpered against his mouth, afraid that the heat building in her body would burn them up. She tried to pull away, afraid of what he was making her feel, but he tightened his grip on her. She clutched at his face, knowing if he let her go she'd fall to the floor, boneless with need.

"I want you to come for me, Ember. Give me that."

She rocked her hips against his hand, and that small concession was enough to trip the trigger. Release rocked through her body, making her cry out as she ripped her mouth from his. Her knees gave way, but he had already released her hair to wrap an arm around her back. He supported her as aftershocks rolled through her, one after another.

When she eventually looked up, he grinned at her. His satisfied expression made her laugh. "You look very smug."

He laughed with her, pulling her into his arms. She felt him press a kiss against her head. She wrapped her arms around his waist to keep herself anchored, inhaling his spicy scent.

"You know, I u-u-used to be really good at pleasing women. And that's not ego. I had a lot of practice when I was y-y-young and good looking."

She pulled back enough to look up at him, intrigued. "Really?" She stepped back, holding one of his hands. "I think you need to show me. Again."

Zeke looked down at her hand in his own, then up to her face. "You n-n-need to be sure, Ember. And you need to be aware, this is n-not a one night thing. If you l-l-l-l-let me in now, I'm going to be here a w-while."

She continued to tow him through the living room and down the hallway to her room. "Good," she whispered.

CHAPTER SIX

EKE DIDN'T KNOW what scared him more: the look in her eyes or the realization that he was about to have sex for the first time in four years. *Definitely the look.*

He could not have changed the course of his feet if he tried, though.

Ember tugged him down the hallway, only pausing long enough to peek in at her sleeping son. She shut Drew's door securely and when they entered her own bedroom, she engaged the lock beside the door knob. Zeke knew the flimsy little piece of metal wouldn't be enough to keep him out, but hopefully it would a child.

They stepped into the bedroom and his disbelief intensified. She was going to do it. Him. As if he were normal, and not some fucked up science experiment. She said the scars and the stuttering didn't bother her, but he didn't understand how they *couldn't.* They sure as hell bothered him. Every damn hour of every day.

She turned to face him at the edge of the bed. The light from the open bathroom door was just enough to show him the insecurity on her face. Her hands tangled in front of her stomach and he was struck with how nervous she was.

"It's n-not too late to change your mind."

She blinked up at him, and smiled. "I'm not going to change my mind, I'm just not sure how to start."

Taking his courage in hand, he stepped forward and settled his lips onto hers. She moaned, curling her fist into his shirt. He liked that one small action of hers, because it magnified how tiny she was compared to him. He dwarfed most of the population, and the attention that brought made him extremely uncomfortable now. During his football years, he'd relished the attention.

Years ago. A lifetime ago.

He loved impressing Ember with his size.

Zeke rested his hand on the curve of her hip, his thumb finding its way beneath the edge of her sweatshirt. He pulled away from her mouth. "C-c-can I take this off?"

She nodded and he peeled it up over her head. The sheet of her dark hair shone in the light as it swayed around her body. Without his urging, she reached behind herself and unfastened the white bra, flinging it aside. Zeke almost nutted in his jeans when he saw her plump breasts for the first time.

They were perfect. Dark pink nipples puckered in the coolness of the room, begging for attention. Reaching out, he brushed against the bottom swell, still half thinking he was in a dream and she was going to shut him down at any second. But she didn't. She leaned into his touch just like she did before, moaning. Using both hands, he cupped her breasts, rubbing his thumbs over the tips. A shiver coursed through her and she grabbed his wrists.

A bolt of mindless fear hit him, because he didn't want her to push him away. If she wasn't ready for this, he would force himself to step away, though it would quite possibly kill him. Instead, she pressed his palms to her even harder, making him thankful he'd found her all over again.

He looked down as he pressed her breasts up and together. His mouth watered at the thought of taking her into his mouth.

Zeke knelt in front of her, glad of his height because it put him at mouth level with her chest. Replacing his hands with his lips, he sucked her nipple deep into his mouth. Ember cried out and wrapped her arms around his head, scraping her fingernails back through his scalp. His stomach bottomed out yet again when he realized she had to be feeling the ridges of his scars underneath his hair, but she didn't even seem to notice. She clutched him to her and pressed kisses to the top of his head.

Zeke hesitated, letting her nipple go. Emotion made his eyes burn. The unrelenting loneliness he normally fought had been pushed away by her slender arms and the cushion of her body. He rested his forehead against her, wanting to soak in the moment.

Ember seemed to understand because her movements slowed, then stopped completely, until she just held him to her.

He felt like a pussy, letting her cradle him like this, but he'd missed being close to another person. Talking to them without the fear they were going to cringe from his looks, or history, or, God forbid, because *they* were uncomfortable.

He hated feeling like he had to apologize for the way he looked. He'd served his country with pride, and done a lot of shit that nobody else would.

The woman in front of him had never given him reason to feel inferior. In anything.

Leaning away from her touch, he started to unfasten her blue jeans. She shuddered as his hands brushed against the smooth skin of her belly. Spreading the zipper placket, he pressed a kiss just above the elastic band of her underwear, then started to tug her jeans down over her hips.

Beautiful. Exactly as he expected her to be. Her belly was slightly rounded and a few faint silver lines marred the perfection of her skin. He pressed kisses to everything he revealed. Desperate impatience threatened to speed his actions, but he was going to take his time. It had been years since he'd been with a woman; he planned to prolong this as long as humanly possible.

As he dragged her jeans down her thighs, she rested a hand on his shoulder to balance when she stepped out of them. Zeke groaned as he caught sight of the wet spot on the light blue cotton of her panties. Unable to do otherwise, he gripped her hips in his hands and dragged her to his mouth, inhaling the scent of her earlier release. He ripped her underwear away and paused to dance his fingers through the dark silky hair. "B-beautiful."

Using one finger to part her folds, he groaned at the slick heat that encased him. There was no way on Earth that that kind of arousal could be duplicated, and it told him more strongly than anything else that she was attracted to him. No matter the scars. No matter the stuttering.

He glided his finger forward in her heat until he found her clit, distended and ready for more attention. Making slow, subtle circles, he taunted her as he refocused his mouth to her pouting breasts. Her hips started to shift in time with his movements, and he could sense when she neared her peak. Drawing his finger down, he angled it up into the depths of her body.

Ember moaned and sagged against him. "Yes, that's where I need you. Please."

Zeke plunged his finger into her body, focusing on the spot just behind her pelvic bone that caused so much pleasure. As her body began to move faster, nearing orgasm, he pulled away.

He ached with need to taste her, to be inside her, but he wanted her release again. By the time he was done with her, she wouldn't care what he looked like.

Pushing to his feet, he lifted her in his arms and took the few steps to the bed. He laid her diagonally across the mattress, then stepped away long enough to rid himself of his own clothes. He was glad for the cover of night, because his body wasn't what it used to be. Yes, he kept in shape, but the aftereffects from that explosion could be seen all over his skin.

Shrapnel scars, surgery scars on his thigh where they'd inserted the rod.

Those worries faded away, though, as she opened her

arms to him. He took long enough to sheath himself with a condom from his wallet and he was on her. Kissing her lips, he nibbled his way down her neck and chest, relishing in her scent, then down the center line of her abdomen. Zeke felt her breath catch as he hovered over the moist heat at the apex of her thighs. She shifted beneath him, her body hungry for what he could provide. Shifting further down, he used his palms to spread her lean thighs.

God she was beautiful. The light from the bathroom glistened on the soft pink folds of her sex, and his mouth watered. Shifting, he laved his tongue up the length of her slit. She tasted as wonderful as he'd dreamed.

Ember shifted her hips on the mattress. Zeke leaned to the side to make room for his hand. As he fondled her clit with his tongue, he rocked two fingers deep into her body, stroking her G-spot hard.

With a wailing cry she tried to stifle with a fist, she convulsed on the bed, fighting to pull away. Spanning her hips with his forearm to hold her in place, Zeke continued to swirl his tongue, sending her crying into another release. As aftershocks shuddered through her body, he kissed his way up to her mouth, aligning their hips. His cock seemed to sense where it needed to go, because it slid to the hilt with one easy push.

Zeke paused above her, afraid to move. With that one immersion, he was on the edge of oblivion.

Ember wrapped her arms around his head and pressed kisses down his jaw to his neck. Her delicate teeth nipped the skin of his clavicle and he knew he had to move. He pulled back, then surged into her again.

In response, she wrapped her sleek legs around his hips and rocked her pelvis up into him. She moaned and he felt the ripple of her internal muscles as she orgasmed yet again, and he was done. With three hard surges, he let the billowing heat consume him, unable to stave it off any longer. The hardest, purest pleasure he'd ever experienced arched his back and he tried to muffle the shout in his throat.

Pure white light overwhelmed his vision as he rode out his body's movements. His arms eventually gave out and he buried his face against her hair as he tried to drag oxygen into his quivering body.

"Holy hell," Ember whispered. Her voice was raspy and he took immense satisfaction in that.

An aftershock rippled through her body, tightening her sheath around him. Zeke groaned as his relaxing cock twitched and he had to surge into her again. She was just too damn good. But the need hadn't been appeased. Already, he could feel the want building inside him for a second round.

She pressed kisses to the side of his neck and jaw, and Zeke knew she wanted him to turn to her. Hardening his heart, preparing for the worst, he lifted his head enough to look her in the eye.

She had one of the most sublime, perfect smiles on her face. Even with the bruise shadowing her cheek, she was beautiful.

And she was looking at him as if he'd hung the moon.

Zeke shifted, uncomfortable with her scrutiny, even after what they'd just shared. Or maybe because of what they'd just shared.

"I had no idea," she murmured. "That was phenomenal. You were phenomenal."

He blinked, unused to hearing anything of the kind for years. He disengaged from her body and sat on the edge of the bed, his reality shifting in his mind.

"Are you okay?"

He glanced at her over his shoulder. "I am."

And he truly was. When he'd been younger, it had been no big deal to sleep around with whomever he'd wanted. But all of those girls faded into obscurity as he looked at Ember curled on her side behind him. She was backlit by the bathroom light, and the hourglass curve of her hip made him want to reach out and feel her smooth skin. There was a blemish on her belly and another on her neck. He scraped his hand over his beard in guilt.

He stood up from the bed and padded into the bathroom to dispose of the condom, then turned to stand at the vanity. His ugly mug looked the same, but he certainly felt different. As trite as it was to think, something had shifted inside him. Or maybe it was just the release of actual sex for the first time in forever.

Turning on the cold water, he washed his hands and splashed his face, trying to delay returning to the bedroom. She would be waiting for him, and he wasn't sure how he felt about what just happened. Yes, he was satisfied. Kind of. The stirrings for another round of play were getting sharper. Emotionally, he didn't know what he felt. He wanted more, definitely. But he was struggling not to feel indebted to her for fucking him. Clothes hid the worst of the damage to his body, but his face was out there for everybody to see. Yet she'd still taken him. *Why* kept echoing through his head.

Straightening, wishing he had an ounce of the confidence that he did when he was a kid, he walked out of the bathroom.

Ember was curled up on her side, the sheet draped over her lightly. Her hands were folded beneath her unbruised cheek, eyes closed. They fluttered open when she heard him come out, and his heart jumped in his chest at the way she smiled at him. There was no guile there, that he could see.

He heard a familiar beep coming from his jeans pocket, and he scanned the room for a clock. When he spied one on her bedside table, he cursed. "I was supposed to be at work half an hour ago."

Ember frowned and seemed upset as he started to move around the room, gathering his clothes. She sat up on the side of the bed and dragged the sheet around her. "Is there anything I can do to help?"

He grabbed his phone from his jeans pocket as he slid them up his legs. Chad, asking where he was.

Ember blinked up at him, and he felt like an ass. "I'm s-sorry. I didn't exp-pect to do this tonight. I have to get to work."

Giving him an understanding look, she nodded. "Okay. I'm sorry you're late."

He shrugged, turning his face away. "No big deal.

Chad will stay until I get there."

She sat cross-legged on the bed as he pulled on the rest of his clothes. She didn't nag at him or force him to talk, and as he prepared to leave, he knew she wouldn't say a word if he walked out the door without acknowledging her at all. But he couldn't do that. Crossing to stand before her, he leaned down to press a kiss to her forehead. She tipped her mouth up, though, and his lips landed on hers. Need surged, and it took everything he had to pull away. "I have to go."

She sighed, smiling up at him. "Okay. But before you do I need you to know that tonight was very special to me. I've never felt anything like what you gave me. Didn't even know it was possible. So, thank you."

Zeke tipped his head to her and walked out the door, too overwhelmed with emotion to form a response. Satisfaction fought with relief that he'd been able to bring her pleasure. It had been so long he'd feared not being able to satisfy her. Locking the front door behind himself, he jogged to his truck through the swirling snow, feeling almost joyous. Lighter than he'd felt in a very long time.

Chad grinned when he saw him pull into the LNF parking lot and get out of his truck. Ants marched across his scalp and he felt color surge through his face at the scrutiny. Hopefully, the night concealed most of it. "What?" he demanded.

"I'm not going to bitch at you because it looks like you had better things on your mind than a boring stakeout. I hope you tucked her into bed nicely before you left."

Zeke snorted and grimaced in spite of himself. "Kind of."

Chad nodded as he handed over keys to the nondescript black Crown Vic they'd been using for surveillance on the Malone case. "It was quiet, as always. Our contract is up soon and her ex is going to be pissed we have nothing to report."

He nodded his head in agreement. "I know. I've n-never seen anything going on there. That woman lives like a h-h-hermit."

Chad rubbed his hand over his face and looked at the office building. Snow swirled through the vapor light. "Well, we'll work the contract and file our report, but he's isn't going to like what we have to say."

Zeke shook his head, gathering his lunchbox from the truck. "Nope."

"You still on for next Monday?"

The bottom fell out of his stomach as he remembered the date. Fuck. It had slipped his mind. "I g-guess."

Chad smacked him on the shoulder. "I'll be right there with you."

He nodded, throat tight. It was amazing that he'd found this group of men, willing to take him in, warts and all, so to speak. Chad kept better track of his schedule than he did. The fact that he'd remembered Zeke's surgery and Zeke hadn't was disturbing.

The quiet night gave him too much time to think about what had happened with Ember. They'd moved too fast, he knew that. But for the life of him he didn't think he'd change it if he could go back. She'd rocked his world. In spite of all his misgivings, she hadn't made him feel like a pity fuck.

His phone buzzed in his pocket. Shielding the illumination with his jacket to maintain cover, he pulled up the screen.

Wish we'd had more time.

His heart rate sped up and heat raced into his groin.

Me too.

He dragged in a deep breath, debating what to write. The darkness gave him false courage. *Maybe next time we'll have longer.*

Definitely! ;-)~

Oorah! That sounded like a promise. Slipping his phone into his pocket, he leaned back against the seat. She was tying him in knots. And he loved it.

CHAPTER SEVEN

EMBER WAS A bit tender the next day, but she relished it. Not only had she made love with an awesome guy, he'd kind of promised to see her again. She glanced at the neon clock on the grill wall, and realized she'd been polishing the same brass rail for the better part of ten minutes. There weren't many customers right now, but she still felt her cheeks flush with embarrassment.

Zeke consumed her thoughts. Even though she had so many other things she needed to think about and work on, he was always center stage. She wondered if he was sleeping, or working out. Sweat glistening across his chest.

She looked down at the hand clenched on the rag. If she wasn't careful, she was going to hurt herself.

The little crush she'd had on him had definitely grown, exponentially it seemed like. When he walked into a room, he made her feel alive. Her heart rate picked up, nervousness invaded her system. It was as if she were in high school again. Although most high-schoolers had more experience than she did with the opposite sex.

Men hit on her all the time when she worked, but the attention turned into the buzz of bees after a while;

irritating but no immediate danger. She'd never been tempted by any of the smooth talking men that came in.

Maybe the fact that Zeke wasn't a smooth-talker at all was the pull.

The front door opened and the man of her dreams walked through. She grinned when she met his gaze, and he returned her smile, sending her heart into palpitations. She glanced at the clock on the wall. "You're up early."

He shrugged his broad shoulders. "I couldn't sleep."

His head tipped forward and she followed his line of sight to the front of his jeans. And the blatant erection straining the fabric.

Ember's mouth watered and she cleared her throat. She crossed her arms over her suddenly hard-nippled breasts. "So, you thought you'd, uh, come for a booty call?"

The look he gave her was playful and shamefaced all at the same time, and it was the cutest expression she'd ever seen on his face. Without a second thought, she stepped into his space and leaned up for a kiss.

Zeke seemed shocked at first, then thrilled, and he threw himself into it. His heavy hand gripped her hip to pull her into his hardness and Ember pushed against him. It wasn't until somebody cleared their throat beside them that they realized where they were and what they were doing.

Katy, one of the waitresses, stood to their side, blocking the view from some customers. "We have a couple kids here," she whispered.

Ember felt embarrassment ruddy her skin and pulled

away. She glanced over Katy's shoulder and sure enough, two parents were glaring at her and trying to distract their kids with crayons.

For a wild moment, Ember didn't care. She wanted to kiss Zeke until forever, right here.

But right here was not the right place.

"Sorry, Katy. I'm going to take my lunch break. Think you can handle the rabid crowd?"

Katy gave her a 'you're crazy' look and glanced around the deserted restaurant. "I think I'll be able to handle it."

Zeke was just as embarrassed and happy to follow along behind as she pushed through the swinging door to the kitchen. The cook was at a counter in the corner, prepping vegetables for the evening service, and didn't even glance up when they walked in, down the aisle and into her office. Ember dragged Zeke inside then locked the door behind him.

He didn't let her turn around.

His bearded face nestled into the hollow of her neck, and she shuddered as chills raced across her skin from the contact. The elastic band holding the braid down the middle of her back fell to her feet, and her hair unraveled. Zeke buried his nose in it, breathing her in, and pressed his groin into her ass. "You've d-d-drugged me. I couldn't think of anything but you last night and this morning."

Ember gasped at the move and instinctively pushed back against him. Arousal burned through her body, exciting her beyond coherence. She gasped, her forehead pressed to the door and arched her back against him.

Zeke shifted, running his hands up her ribcage beneath her shirt to her breasts. Plumping them together, he scraped his thumbnails over the tips until she moaned out his name. He peppered kisses all over the unhurt side of her face. Ember twisted her head around enough to meet his lips, more thankful than she'd ever been that she had her own office, away from prying eyes. What she was doing was bad. Definitely not how a business owner should behave.

There was no way she was going to stop.

His massive hands left her breasts and cupped her hips, guiding her movements against his cock. Ember cried out and flexed her legs, trying to get closer. "I need you in me."

She shoved her black pants down her legs, and she heard Zeke unzip his jeans. As she kicked her pants and shoes away, she realized she dripped with arousal. Her clit throbbed, ached to be touched and fondled. But her sheath needed filled, desperately. That's what she really wanted. She felt empty without him.

Again, she tried to turn around, but he stopped her. "This way." One broad hand pushed against her back and she lowered her head. She would have felt embarrassed if he hadn't immediately slipped the head of his cock inside her body. She groaned, and tried to take him deeper, but he gripped her hips in his hands to hold her still. Then he began to play.

Stroking only about an inch inside her body, he angled to provide her the most pleasure. With shallow plunges, he played her body with his own as if he'd been doing it forever. Nerve endings exploded in her womb, and her knees almost gave out as the sudden climax washed over her. Ember gripped the door handle and tried not to make so much noise that the cook could hear.

While she was still riding that crest, he pushed through her folds and seated himself as deeply as he could. Ember moaned and shifted. At this angle, with his size, it was more than bordering on uncomfortable. Even as wet as she was, accommodating him took everything she had.

Then he started to move. The initial discomfort faded away, and she found herself bracing against the door to force him into even sharper contact. Breasts swaying, legs quivering, she met him stroke for stroke. Her body reached for another release, relishing in the pounding that had started to send shudders through her limbs. She moaned as another, deeper orgasm crashed into her, and her legs finally did give out.

Zeke wrapped his arms around her and held her through the aftershocks. Once she'd calmed, he lifted her upright, disengaging them only for as long as it took him to cross to the couch. Positioning himself in the center of the cushions, he guided her to sit onto his lap. He tried to keep her facing away, but Ember resisted. "No, I want to turn."

She straddled his hips with her knees, reaching down to guide his heavy cock into her as she sank down. They both gasped as she hit bottom, then squeezed down tighter. Ember leaned forward to wrap her arms around Zeke's neck as she pressed kisses to his bearded jaw line. Zeke cupped her head and brought their mouths together, arching up beneath her at the same time. Crying out, she adjusted her rhythm over top of him, moving quickly from light, shallow bouncing to deep, full-length plunges. She glided her tongue inside his mouth, trying to get as close as she physically could.

Zeke began to lose his reciprocating rhythm, and she knew he was close. His hands held her hips as he sped her movements even faster, using his strength to make tiny adjustments. Ember pulled away from his mouth, unable to contain a high keen as he brought her to pleasure yet again.

As if her release brought on his own, Zeke's intensity stalled as pleasure overwhelmed him. His head dropped to the back of the couch and the veins strained in his neck as he cried out, slamming into her sharply a few more times before melting into the cushions of the couch.

Ember collapsed against his sweaty T-shirted chest to catch her breath, more satisfied than she could ever remember being. Tremors rippled through her muscles and she knew her thighs would be killing her the next day, but she wouldn't have changed anything. She opened her eyes to the file cabinet in her office. Okay, maybe she would have changed the location.

Even that was a lie, though, because knowing that anybody could walk by and hear them had been exhilarating. A restaurant was not the best place to have sex, but she was sure they weren't the only ones to ever do it.

Muscles shifted beneath her as Zeke laid them full out on the couch. She disengaged from his body and found herself laying mostly on his chest. He was too broad to leave her any space on the cushions. But he was surprisingly comfortable, and she felt herself sinking into him.

"I, uh," he cleared his throat, "ap-p-preciate you having s-s-sex. With me."

Ember snorted and rolled her head enough to look up at him. "What do you mean? Here at the grill?"

He shook his head, looking like he'd rather be anywhere else right now. He tipped his chin up, once, to bring her attention to his face. "Because of this. I'm not what you normally see working here."

The pain in his voice broke her heart, but his words made her mad. "No, you're not. If you were, we certainly wouldn't be here."

When his jaw clamped shut and he levered them both up, she realized he'd taken her words completely wrong again. She scrambled to hold him still, but it was like trying to hold a freight train. "Stop, damn it! Zeke, you've got to stop taking everything I say as an insult to your looks."

He hesitated, but avoided her eyes.

"If you were like every other guy that came through here, I would have been completely turned off. None of them do a thing for me, because after meeting you they all seem exceedingly shallow." She leaned into his line of sight. "Again, I like the way you look. No, I fucking love the way you look. Nothing about these scars turn me off in the slightest." She ran her hand over the deepest one cutting across his forehead, and down his cheek. His beard tickled her fingers as she brushed them over his lips. "They are a tiny part of the man you are."

He stared at her, as if trying to right the reality as he thought he knew it. She leaned forward and pressed a kiss to his lips, and his arms slowly came around her. Ember almost cried in relief.

"I have more surgeries coming up, so I won't always look like this."

She shook her head at his stubbornness. Pulling back, she glared at him. "If you need the surgeries for a medical reason, that's fine, but it would kind of break my heart, because I've fa-, uh, gotten used to you this way."

Panic raced through her as she realized she'd almost told him she'd fallen for him.

She had.

The thought didn't scare the crap out of her like she expected. It was a solid, burning glow in her chest, unlike anything she'd ever felt before. She'd felt a version of it for her son and her dad, but this was different. Vital and needed, it almost felt, dare she say it, fated. She didn't have good luck with the opposite sex, but she knew in her gut she was supposed to be with this man.

He shifted beneath her and she realized they were still sitting half naked on her office couch. She glanced at the clock on the wall and groaned. "I was supposed to be back from lunch ten minutes ago. It's Katy's turn."

She scrambled from his lap, but had to stop and stare as he removed the condom with a paper towel, his glorious cock glistening. Zeke's body was the stuff of wet dreams, from the biceps the size of her calves to the cobbled contours of his stomach. There were other scars across his body, but his head and face had obviously taken the brunt of the wall coming down on him.

It broke her heart that the big former Marine was so defensive about his looks.

Ember cleaned up as well as she could and redressed. "We need to work on our timing. Seems like we keep doing this right before one of us has to work. Maybe we can be really crazy someday and have an actual date."

Zeke snorted and stood to pull his jeans up his hips. Ember sighed as he tucked himself away. Once he was dressed, he moved in front of her and lowered his head for a kiss. She let him push responsibility away for a few more minutes, then reluctantly let him go.

"I'm going to go work out."

She nodded. "Yes, you need to. You're looking scrawny."

He grinned at her and wrapped an arm around her ribcage, swinging her high off her feet. Ember squealed in spite of herself and laughed out loud.

"Put me down, damn it!"

Zeke dropped her to her feet and planted a smacking kiss on her lips before letting her go.

"You want to come over for dinner, tonight?"

He paused, eyebrows raised in surprise. "I'd love to."

"Why don't you come over about six, then?"

He smiled at her fully, and she had to catch her breath at the pure happiness she saw shining there. It made her happy the she could make him that happy.

The rest of the day dragged slowly. She wanted to rush home and get ready, but she still had several hours of work yet. Once her shift ended and she handed it over to Deena, she turned for the grocery store. She had no idea what to make him, but she had a feeling anything beef would be good. London broil. With a baked potato and sides.

Drew was ecstatic that Zeke was coming for dinner. The little boy had already developed a significant crush on the big man, and as the time crept closer to six they were both watching the clock.

She picked at the fabric of the blue dress she'd put on. Overkill, probably, but the color reminded her of Zeke's eyes. And she'd taken the time to curl her long hair. It bounced as she walked, and made her feel extra feminine.

When the doorbell finally rang, Drew raced for the door and flung it open. Snow blew into the entryway and Zeke stepped inside quickly, sealing it closed behind himself. He started to brush himself off when he glanced up at her and froze.

Ember shifted as he surveyed her from the top of her curled bangs to the tip of her shoes without saying a word. Her cheeks heated with embarrassment. Definitely overkill.

Then he started to walk toward her, emotion filling his gaze.

"You dressed up for me?"

Ember blinked at the deep whisper, as if he didn't want Drew to hear. She nodded and pushed some of her hair behind her ear. "I know it's just us, but I thought we could make it feel like a date."

His lips tipped up in a smile. "I'm...f-f-fl...." He stopped, closing his eyes and taking a breath. "Thank you. If I had known I would have d-d-dressed up as well."

She grinned and leaned up for his kiss. "I don't think they make dresses your size," she whispered.

He tipped back his head and laughed out loud. Drew squeezed in between them to see what they were laughing at. Ember told him and his eyes widened dramatically, then he dissolved into knee-slapping giggles.

They had a wonderful dinner together, and she could see Drew falling in love with Zeke. At one point she sat back and tried to survey the situation from a protective mother's standpoint, rather than a woman falling in love. Was she creating a dynamic that would or could hurt her child? Was she looking at the relationship between she and Zeke responsibly?

Unfortunately, the answer to both questions was unequivocally yes.

She would never intentionally hurt Drew, but she couldn't make herself consider shutting Zeke out. It would feel like trying to cut off her own arm.

Interestingly, Zeke seemed just as fascinated with Drew. When they disappeared after dinner, she wandered through the apartment looking for them and followed the rumble of voices to her son's room.

They were both sprawled on their bellies playing Legos, dark head tucked trustingly in next to the dirty blond.

Zeke shifted his booted feet as Drew patted him on the shoulder for something, and she was struck by how involved they were. She stepped into the room to draw their attention and motioned to the clock on his dresser. "You need to get ready for bed, buddy."

His little face puckered up to argue but Zeke bumped him in the shoulder with his fist. "Good playing with you, buddy."

Drew's dark head nodded and he trudged into the bathroom to brush his teeth.

Ember smiled as Zeke gathered Legos by the handful to drop into the blue container. "Thank you for playing with him. My dad is usually the one doing this stuff with him. Drew's kind of at loose ends right now."

Zeke shifted his broad shoulders in a shrug. "I-I-I had fun, too."

His blue eyes tracked up her legs, up her thighs and settled on her breasts, put on display by the fitted bodice of the dress. "Do you want to play?"

Ember looked at the devilment dancing in his eyes and doubted she could deny this man anything. "Perhaps."

The seed was sown, though, because as she looked at him sitting cross-legged on the floor, the thought chased through her mind that she could straddle him right there and ride him into oblivion. Awareness crept across her skin, and she took a step forward.

Drew jumped in front of her and peeled his lips back to show her he'd scrubbed his teeth. Ember laughed, leaning down to wrap her son in her arms. How could she have forgotten where she was? "Looks good, buddy."

Her eyes flicked to Zeke as he pushed to his feet, power in every movement. A shiver coursed through her body as she remembered all that intensity lunging up beneath her, satisfying them both. She urged Drew to climb into bed and tucked him in, with a kiss on his forehead.

Zeke moved to the door.

"Wait. I liked having you here. Will you come over again?"

The big man seemed surprised but nodded, ducking his head as he slipped through the doorway.

Ember brushed her hand through her son's hair. "That was very nice of you to invite him back."

Snuggling under the blankets, he blinked up at her sleepily. "He needs a family. Maybe ours. He doesn't have anybody out here."

Her lips curved at his sweet little heart. "Maybe you're right. We'll see, buddy. I love you. Have good dreams."

As she pulled the door closed behind her, the tension in her body began to hum. Dishes clanked in the kitchen, so she headed in that direction.

Zeke was unloading her dish drainer, going through

cupboards until he found the right place for things.

"You don't have to do that."

He glanced at her from beneath his hair and shrugged. "M-might as well. We always pitched in when I was a kid."

"Do you have brothers and sisters?" she asked curiously.

He nodded. "Two of each. I'm the second youngest."

She raised her brows at him. "And are they still all on the farm?"

Sighing, he shrugged. "K-k-kind of. They all live within a few miles of one another, sharing resources and la-la-lab," he stopped to take a breath. "They all work together. I've moved the farthest away."

Ember so wished she could do something to help him out with his words. At least he wasn't stuttering as much as when she'd first met him.

"You were really nervous when you started coming into the grill. Was that all because of me?"

He looked at her out of the corner of his eye. "W-w-why would you think y-you made me n-n-n-n-nervous?"

When she grinned at him and raised her brows, bumping his arm with her shoulder, he cursed. "Partly. It's crowds, in general. R-raises our anxiety l-level. And I'm not like I used to b-be."

"Physically, you mean?" He handed her a pan to put away.

They had reached the end of the dishes, and he didn't seem to know what to do with his hands. Turning to lean against the sink, he sank his hands into his pockets. Ember moved to lean against the opposite counter, almost mirror to his position, though she folded her arms beneath her breasts.

"I started playing football w-when I was a kid. All through school. High school, I started to ser-ser...really grow." He spread his arms expansively. "The physical stuff came easy to me. They made me quarterback and I was popu-ular. Won state and national championships." Crossing his arms, he stared off into his memories.

"School was easy for me." He winked at her. "So w-were the girls. I had a bit of a reputation as a p-party guy. But it got boring."

Ember cocked a brow at him. "You got tired of women falling all over you? What kind of kid were you?"

Grinning, he shrugged his heavy shoulders and shifted his stance, looking a little shamefaced. "Okay, m-maybe I didn't mind that so much, but after a while it got m-mo-mo...tiring. My parents wanted me to wo-work with them, and I couldn't. I graduated school and immediately enlisted in the Marines."

"Were they hurt?"

He sighed. "A bit. They thought I would get killed. Which, I almost did."

Ember didn't like to hear him talk like that. Her stomach turned at the thought of him never coming home. He was such a strong, vital force that she just couldn't imagine it.

"Did they gloat?"

His eyes flickered.

"Not exactly. I got the whole 'if you had stayed on the farm' thing." He shrugged. "I went home for a while after I got out of the hospital be-be-because I still had a lot of rehab to do. But I was r-restless. A friend told me about LNF and I sent them a resume. I didn't know any of the guys while I was in the Marines, but I was in the same Company Chad and Duncan had left. Duncan c-called for me to come for an…in-interview and they welcomed me in like I'd always been with them."

"Wow." That was so impressive.

"I was a m-m-mess when I started. But they still saw something in me and hired me." He shrugged and made a face. "They let me off when I need to go in for p-p-procedures, or rehab. If I need to have surgery they give me w-work I can do in the hospital and home if I feel up to it. I don't know if any other job would be so under-standing as LNF."

Ember's stomach felt off.

"Do you have more surgeries coming up?"

He shrugged his shoulders and looked at his boots. "Reconstr-r-ructive stuff. I have a few more to go."

It was obviously not something he wanted to talk about, so she shifted topic. "What are you doing for Christmas?"

He looked up to scan her face. "Nothing really. I'm supposed to go to J-john and Shannon's house at some point. He's one of the partners and Shannon is our o-o-office manager."

Ember chewed the inside of her lip. "Well, you're welcome to come over here too. We're going to be opening presents and my dad may come over at some point. Frog Dog is open a half day tomorrow, then closed on Christmas."

His face warmed with a smile. "I appreciate the invitation. I don't want to be a pest."

"Oh, please," she snorted. "I love having you here."

For a long moment, he didn't say anything, but the feeling in the room changed. "I love being here."

Ember stepped into the space between his spread feet and leaned up for a kiss. Zeke immediately wrapped his arms around her back to pull her snug against him.

The arousal that had been simmering in the air spiked, and Ember's nipples became sensitized. She brushed her breasts against his chest, wishing their clothes were already gone. She felt Zeke swell into her belly.

"We have a few hours, right?"

He nodded against her mouth and slipped his tongue inside. She moaned as he cupped her head and forced her to take him all in. Ember decided then and there that he was the best thing she'd ever tasted. She wondered if he tasted like that all over. Pulling away she pressed kisses down his scruffy jaw, down his corded neck and to the collar of his T-shirt. Running her hands beneath the fabric, she pushed it up to his shoulders. Zeke pulled it over his head and dropped it to the kitchen floor.

Ember sighed as she ran her hands over the hard contours of his upper body. She already knew he worked out a lot, and it was very evident in the way his muscles were cut. Dirty blond hair covered his chest and darkened in the cleft between his pecs. A narrow trail cut through the center of his abs, and she desperately wanted to explore.

The kitchen wasn't necessarily the best place to do what she wanted to do.

She grabbed his hand and backed away, tugging him through the doorway and down the hall. She closed her bedroom door behind them and motioned to the bed. "Sit down, please."

In the dim light from the bedside lamp, his blue eyes heated and he grinned as he did what she asked.

Ember reached for the zipper under her arm and tugged it down, slowly revealing the black teddy she wore beneath. Zeke sucked in a breath as she let the dress fall to the floor, and his hands curled into the comforter. "You wore that for me?"

Smiling, she took a step toward him. He immediately cupped her breasts then ran his hands down her sides to her hips. His touch through the satin felt phenomenal, and distracting. Lowering herself to the floor, she wedged herself between his knees and began to unfasten his belt and jeans. His eyes closed and he leaned back on his braced arms to give her room to work.

Ember had never done this for a man before, but she wanted to learn what made him yearn for release. He made her come so easily, she wanted to do the same for him.

When his pants were unfastened, she stood long enough to tug them down his legs, then went back to her knees to admire the stretched blue cotton of his briefs.

Dancing her fingers over his substantial length, she tried to be patient, but greed now controlled her movements. They didn't have very long and she wanted to enjoy him.

When she peeled the cotton away from Zeke's penis, it stood straight and proud up from his hips. Roped with heavy veins, it was flushed dark pink with blood flow. Her mouth watered. Leaning forward, she pressed an openmouthed kiss to the underside of the fleshy, purplish head, making it flex. She wrapped her right hand around the base and licked up from her thumb, confirming her earlier thought. Sweet. But musky, too. Definitely masculine.

Wrapping her lips completely around the head, she ran the tip of her tongue into the crease in the middle. Zeke groaned and met her eyes. "Fuck, Ember."

The exclamation made her smile, as she pulled up. "Like that do you?"

"God, yes."

Spreading her lips she swallowed him again, this time working down his length. She tried to meet the hand at the base with her lips, but he was a little too long to do that comfortably. So she started to work her hand up as her mouth went up.

Zeke groaned and fell back to the bed, clutching the bedspread beside his hips. As her mouth rode his length, he began to twitch beneath her. His legs shifted restlessly.

Ember had never been so turned on in her life. The fact that she could do this to him—this huge, strong man—empowered her like nothing she'd ever done before.

She bobbed faster, intent on bringing him the same pleasure he had to her many times over. She tasted salty fluid on her tongue and almost orgasmed herself. He was getting close.

When he wrapped his hands into her long hair and began to guide her movements, thrusting up into her mouth, Ember moaned, which seemed to excite him even more. "Fuck, I'm g-going to come. You need to move if you're going to."

She didn't budge.

The first hot flood of his release almost choked her until she timed her swallows with her plunges. He jerked beneath her as if he'd been shot. His fists left her hair and clutched at the comforter as he arched off the bed and moaned. Ember had to move with his body to keep him in her mouth, and it was the raunchiest, most sensual encounter she'd ever taken part in.

Zeke's movements eventually slowed and he sagged into the mattress, panting. Ember gave him one more lingering swirl with her tongue and pulled away. She snagged a towel from the clothes basket on the floor and wiped her hand and mouth, then climbed up onto the bed beside him. She was slick with need, but oddly satisfied with *his* satisfaction. If he wanted to roll over and go to sleep, she would be content.

As he rocked his head to look at her, she had to revise that. Zeke was gloriously relaxed, but there was something in his eyes that told her they were just starting. His body gleamed with sweat and as he rolled off the bed to remove his underwear, the mood in the room changed. The little bit of submission he'd given her was gone, and his jaw clamped with determination as he crawled over her to nestle between her legs, braced on his arms. He had already started to harden again and she was surprised at how easy it seemed to be for him. "I didn't think guys could go like that, one right after another?"

Grinning, he nipped at her lips. "I have a l-l-lot of time to make up for."

Her choked laughed changed to a squeal as he levered down to suck her satin-clad nipple into his hot mouth. One hand reached to unsnap the soaked crotch of her teddy, then his agile fingers were inside her, stroking her hard. Between the atmosphere of the room, her arousal and his determination, it was mere seconds before she started to orgasm against his hand. He wrung every tremor from her he could, and when he replaced his hand with his cock, she was more than ready for him to sink into her.

But he stopped, quivering over top of her, and started to pull away.

"What?"

"Condom."

She didn't want him to leave. She clutched at his shoulders. "Don't go. I'm clean and I have an IUD. I just want you inside me."

Groaning, he rested his head against her breasts. "Are you f-fucking sure? I'm clean too, but I want you to be p-p-positive."

She nodded against the bed and he gave her no more warning. He slammed into her heat and started to piston against her. Ember cried out and widened her legs to take him deeper. She dug her fingernails into the shifting muscles of his ass, urging him on as the bed groaned beneath them.

"You feel as good inside as this does outside." He glided his hand down her hip.

"And you feel massive like this, too big for me to take, but it's just right, too."

His length plunged into her over and over again, and that burning excitement began to build inside her. Then from one stroke to the next he shoved her over that peak.

Ember thought for sure she was going to lose consciousness, the spine-cracking pleasure was so intense. Zeke never gave her a chance to catch her breath. If anything, he plunged harder to reach his own satisfaction. As he reached his own peak, Ember was caught by a secondary orgasm as her body accepted everything his had to give. She held him to her as his body shuddered its release.

When he finally sank into her neck, she was as wrung out, but satisfied as she could be. Even his crushing weight felt right to her. Zeke's hot breath blew her hair as he lifted up enough to look down at her. "Are you okay?"

She nodded, running her hands over every sweaty, muscled inch she could reach. "Hell, yes. May be a little tender in the morning, but I'm getting used to that."

His brows pulled together in concern. "H-h-how tender?"

She cursed herself for making him worry. "Not enough to stop doing this but enough to remind me sometimes throughout the day that I cradled you here. It's very sexy, actually."

The frown deepened. "Why didn't you say something?"

He started to pull out but she tightened her legs around his hips. "Because I had a feeling you'd do this. Go all protective. If I didn't like it, I guarantee you wouldn't be invited back, Zeke. I think with practice," she gave him a little wink, "we'd take care of the tenderness issue. My body is doing things it's only done once before."

Some of the worry faded from his eyes and he pressed a kiss to her lips. "I wouldn't do anything to hurt you. Ever. At least, not deliberately."

Ember nodded. "I know. That's why I'm nuts about you."

His head jerked back and he looked at her sharply. "What?"

She shrugged beneath him. "I'm nuts about you. Love to see your face walk through my doors. Can't wait to talk to you. I feel safe with you."

He blinked heavily, as if he didn't believe the words he heard.

Ember decided she wouldn't tell him she loved him, because if his reaction was any indication, he'd probably panic. He seemed honestly surprised that she would enjoy his company.

"You k-k-know, I'm the same way. You m-make me not feel like a damn freak."

Tears filled her eyes and rolled down her temples. "You're not a freak. You're a courageous man who's been through a lot for his country. People should be going out of their way to meet you and thank you."

He snorted. "I don't know about all that."

She caught his gaze. "I do. And I thank you for going over there and trying to make my life and that of my child better."

He kissed her, as if to soak up her words, then buried his face in the pillow beside her head. From top to bottom and everywhere in between, they were as close as two people could be.

Chapter Eight

ZEKE SHOOK HIS head as he walked out into the cold that night, shocked at the changes that had taken place in the past few days. Ember was amazing. She left him speechless with her words. Probably a good thing. They'd been together such a short time, though, that he had to be leery. She hadn't been with him long enough to know what he went through, with all his surgeries and rehabs. He'd been very careful to not say much about that part of his life.

Christmas fell on a Thursday this year. Tomorrow was Christmas Eve. Four days after that he was scheduled for another reconstructive surgery, his thirteenth.

He hadn't told her anything about it.

Guilt nagged at him. If they were building a relationship, she'd be pissed that he didn't say anything to her about the procedure. But if he did it, and told her later, he would save her a ton of worry.

She didn't need the anxiety right now on top of everything else.

As he headed toward the LNF office, he ran his hand over his head, shoving his hair out of his eyes. In a few days he'd be shaved again, and every line, mark and divot in his head would be out there for the world to see.

Hell.

DUNCAN WAS THE only one in the office when the phone rang the next morning. "Lost 'N' Found Investigative Service."

A voice cleared at the other end. "Is Duncan Wilde in?"

"Speaking."

"Mr. Wilde, this is Detective Angela Holloway, Denver PD. I wanted to talk to you about the report you filed the other night on the missing man."

Duncan limped his way behind his desk and sat down. "Yes. Have you learned anything?"

"No, not really. I just wanted to confirm the information you'd given to Detective Roberts."

The detective asked him a series of questions, and he repeated all that he knew about the homeless former soldier, but it wasn't very much.

Detective Holloway sighed on the other end of the line.

"Well, that matches up with what I have. Unfortunately, I can find no record of an Aiden Willingham being discharged from any of the service branches within the past five years, and no personal information, either. I'm kind of at a dead end. Unless a body turns up or I get a tip, the report will stand as a missing person. I wish I could give you better news."

Duncan frowned and swung the chair to look out his

window. The morning vista was impressive, but he didn't even see it. His eyes scanned the deserted streets.

"I have a feeling," she continued, "that we'll find a body in the next few days. I'll be blunt, Mr. Wilde. That was a lot of blood in that alley. If he had issues like you suggested, it sounds like he may have taken his own life."

Duncan clenched his jaw. He hated to admit it, but the younger vet probably had done something drastic. That kind of blood pool didn't come from a cut finger. It came from somebody deliberately trying to kill or maim. Aiden had been the only one in that alley, as far as they knew.

"I appreciate you calling me, Detective, especially considering it's the holiday."

"Well, all the days run together for me. It was no big deal. I'm sorry I didn't have better news."

"Just," he hesitated. "Just don't give up on this, okay Detective?"

"Oh, I won't, sir. Roberts was ready to close the case, but I took it over. I'll keep my eye on it. I promise."

Duncan hung up, feeling like shit. If he'd only been a little more convincing, or empathetic, or quicker to offer help, maybe Aiden would still be here.

EMBER GOT READY for work happily that day. The grill was only open for a few hours, then they had a day and a half off. Ms. Miller watched Drew. Ember felt bad about using her on a holiday, but the woman seemed to need every penny she could bring in. Two of the kids she watched throughout the day were her own.

She'd told Ember to go ahead and do what she needed to do for Christmas, and Ember made the same offer. So, this afternoon, when she should be getting Christmas ready for Drew, she would be babysitting Ms. Miller's boy and girl.

She couldn't begrudge the time, though, because the woman had seemed ecstatic to get a few hours alone.

Zeke occupied her thoughts throughout the day, and she wracked her brain trying to decide what to get him for Christmas. They hadn't opened the packages he'd given them, so she had no idea how big or little they were.

When he'd been at her dad's house and picked up the guitar, he'd seemed happy. Maybe a song book? She had no idea.

As she wandered through the mall with five million other people later that day, nothing seemed exactly right. She did stumble across a shadow box, though, that she thought would be nice to display her dad's medals in.

Ember finally settled on a T-shirt that said, 'Guitar Players do it better in the dark'. Kind of funny but not too personal. She didn't want him to feel pressured. For laughs, she bought a small Lego set that Drew could help wrap and give him.

Ms. Miller, Erin as she asked Ember to call her, brought her kids over later that afternoon and promised to be back within a couple of hours. And she was. Smiling and tired. The kids had played the entire time, and refused to go home without a fuss. Ember promised them they could come again another day.

It felt strange not seeing Zeke that day, so she sent him a text asking him if he wanted to come for a late dinner. He responded almost immediately that he did, and would be over as soon as he'd showered. Ember made French-bread pizzas that night, not very Christmas-y, but easy and filling. She had just placed them into the oven when he knocked on her door.

As she swung it open, she tried not to appear too eager. But he was freshly showered, and his hair was drawn back into a tight, short ponytail. She hadn't realized it was long enough to do that. Spicy body wash reached her nose and she inhaled, smiling appreciatively. "Damn you smell good."

He made an odd face, like he didn't believe her, but leaned down for a kiss anyway. Ember drew him into her arms and held on as he lifted her off her feet. Kicking the door shut behind him, he carried her into the living room and set her down.

Drew blasted into the room, just as happy to see Zeke as she was. The boy ran to the tree and grabbed the wrapped box of Legos they'd bought him, thrusting them at the big man. "Open your present, Zeke!"

The rattle from inside the box was very distinctive, but he smiled as if he were clueless anyway. His gaze met hers over the boy's head. "Mind if I open my gift?"

She shook her head and waved him to the couch. "Have a seat."

He dropped down into the opposite corner and

ripped into the paper. "Oh, wow," he gushed. "I love these ones!"

Drew beamed as if he'd chosen them himself. "I knew you would!"

He ran to the tree and retrieved his second gift, holding it out to Zeke. "That's just a T-shirt, but Mom said you'd like it."

"Drew!" Ember admonished.

The boy looked shamefaced for a minute, but not very long.

Zeke unwrapped the gift and laughed when it unfolded in front of him. "She's right, I do like it. A lot."

"Can I open the gift you got me now? Please?"

Once again, Zeke looked to her for guidance. She shrugged. "I don't mind."

Drew grabbed both gifts from the top of the pile beneath the tree, practically throwing Ember's at her. She couldn't contain a girlish little thrill of excitement as she started to carefully ease the pretty paper away. Drew squealed when he unwrapped the Spider-Man toy, because it was one he didn't have. After a hurried thank you, he ran into his room to have a superhero fight.

As Ember finally revealed the front of the little box, tears came to her eyes. "Oh," she sighed as she flipped the lid and slid the little figurine out. "It's beautiful."

The little elephant was adorable. He looked like he'd just taken a tumble, and landed splay-legged on the ground. She crossed the room and made a spot for it on top of the entertainment center with the other treasures.

"It looks like it's always been there," she sighed and

sank down onto the couch beside him, pressing a kiss to his lips. "You could not have gotten me anything more perfect. That was my mother's collection first, then I started to add to it. Thank you."

She wrapped her arm around his midsection and leaned into him.

"You're welcome," he whispered, pressing a kiss to the top of her head.

After Drew went to bed early that night, they made love sweetly and curled up together afterwards. "Do you have to leave?" she asked finally.

"No, not i if you don't want me to."

"I would love for you to stay," she whispered, her throat tight with tears.

Ember took long enough to lay out the Santa Claus gifts for Drew, then came back to bed.

Zeke held her all through the night, and it was the most amazing sensation Ember had ever had. She'd never let another man do that for her. She knew Drew would be up in just a few hours, but she couldn't make herself go to sleep.

When she did eventually drift off, it seemed like mere seconds before Drew was bouncing on her bed, urging her up to go open presents. Ember glanced around for Zeke, but didn't see any sign of him. It wasn't until she dressed and headed for the living room that she realized somebody had made coffee.

ZEKE DIDN'T KNOW what his reception would be when Ember walked into the room. They hadn't really made plans to be together on Christmas Day, but it felt right to be in her kitchen right now, cooking breakfast and making coffee. Her sleep tousled hair hung around her face, but he still thought she was the most beautiful thing he'd ever seen. When she walked into his arms for a morning hug, he couldn't help but fall a little in love with her.

A little more, rather.

He hadn't had a lot of relationship experience. Some of the guys he'd served with had girls, wives even, at home waiting for them, but it just hadn't happened for him. Nobody had seriously pinged his radar.

Ember didn't just ping his radar, she damn near crashed his plane. The woman appealed to him in every way she could. Hell, she stood in front of him now with no bra, no make-up, her hair a mess, but she drew him to her like a drug.

As he cradled her in his arms, he couldn't imagine being anywhere else on Earth.

Drew ran in carrying a boxed game. "Mom, look what he brought me!"

They each grabbed a coffee and wandered out to the living room to watch the boy rip open his presents. Her father sent her a text message wishing her a Merry Christmas, and she invited him over to watch Drew play with his new toys. "Do you mind?" she asked him.

Zeke shook his head, knowing it was important for her to have her family together. "Do you want me to go and let you have alone time with your dad?"

If she absolutely wanted that, he would abide by her wishes. But she scrunched up her face and shook her head. "Heck, no. I want all of you to be here. Is that okay?"

"Yes."

And it was.

When Hank arrived later that morning, he seemed tentative in his welcome. Zeke had some issues to work out with Ember's dad, but for the most part he seemed like a good guy. Former Marine, so he wasn't totally bad. It was very evident to see that he loved his daughter and grandson. That love was reciprocated.

When he opened the empty shadow box, tears came to his eyes.

"We found your Purple Heart when I was packing. You should be proud of that. Now it has a place."

Father and daughter cried together, and Zeke felt his own throat tighten with emotion. Maybe if Norton could work through his PTSD issues, he'd be able to be proud of how he'd served his country.

Ember's dad didn't stay long. It was as if he knew he couldn't push it with her. Several times over the morning, Zeke had caught him staring at the fading bruise on her jaw, then looking away. It probably would be hard to look at the evidence of your fucked-up-ness over and over again.

Later that morning, Chad sent a text asking him where he was, and he debated not responding.

Ember's.

You coming over for lunch??? Bring her with you. Shannon would love her.

Zeke frowned, unsure she'd even want to go.

When he mentioned that the guys from LNF were having a get-together, she thought he was trying to leave. "No," he interrupted, "I want you to go with me."

Those damn ants started marching across his scalp again, making his skin prickle, but she didn't seem to notice how embarrassed he was. A brilliant smile spread across her broad mouth. "Really? I'd love to go over with you. Would they mind having a child there?"

Zeke shrugged. Drew would definitely be the only one there, but that would probably get him extra attention, which the little boy dearly loved.

She hopped up from the couch and headed for the door. "I'll get dressed."

An hour later they pulled up in front of John and Shannon's house. There wasn't enough room to park in the driveway crowded with SUVs and trucks, so they parked on the street. Ember had to slide across the seat to Zeke's side because the snowdrift wouldn't allow her to open her door. She smiled happily when he helped her down.

Drew thought they were on a great adventure, and loved the handicapped access ramp at the front of the house. They let him run up and down three times before Ember pulled him to her side. Zeke knocked on the door.

Shannon Murphy was five feet and one inch of sweetness. Zeke smiled when he saw her in her head-to-

toe elf costume and leaned down for his hug.

"Oh, Zeke, wonderful! I didn't think you were coming! And who's this?"

Her gorgeous hazel eyes widened when he introduced Ember and Drew, but she pulled them each into a quick embrace, bells jingling, before letting them go.

"I hope you don't mind Zeke bringing us?" Ember frowned. "I know we're kind of last minute."

Shannon waved her hand. "Oh, don't worry about it. We've got enough for everybody. I just wanted the guys to have a place to go for Christmas because so many of them are away from home. Please, come in and enjoy yourselves."

Zeke had to admit, Ember totally pumped his ego. As he introduced her to most of the guys he worked with, they checked her out with interest. Her hold on his hand or arm kept them from pursuing her.

When he caught sight of John Palmer through the crowd, he snorted with laughter and tugged Ember toward him.

Zeke's hard-ass, second in command boss, former Marine Gunnery Sergeant, wore a Grinch hat, complete with hairy tassel and scowl. Ember giggled and held out her hand. "I'm Ember."

"John Palmer, aka, The Grinch." His hard dark eyes scanned her face. "Zeke take care of whoever did that to you?"

Ember's cheeks turned a little pink, but she nodded. Zeke swallowed heavily. John didn't even hesitate in his assumption that he would step up and do what needed doing.

The faith from one of the men he respected most at the Agency floored him.

When he first started at LNF, he knew he was more fuck-up than actual help, but they'd given him time to settle into a slot he could manage and do well in. They'd accommodated his shortcomings, and used his determination to get the job done right to their advantage. Loyalty had been earned on both sides.

It meant the world to him that he belonged to such a great group of guys.

Chad joined them and held a cookie out to Drew, who hadn't left Ember's side. "Here you go, little man."

Drew looked up at Ember's nod of permission, then quickly snatched the cookie from the man's hand. "Thank you!"

"You're welcome. There's more in the kitchen."

Ember laughed in embarrassment as her son ate the treat in three bites, then headed for more.

"Maybe you shouldn't have told him where they are."

Chad shrugged and ate his own cookie. "He's not going to hurt anything here. Let him have fun. Mind if I talk to Zeke a minute?"

Ember smiled and shook her head, and he was struck with how right it felt to have her here. She didn't seem shocked by anybody's appearance, or look at them with pity. She wandered over to the couch and sat down with Shannon. The two of them were laughing almost immediately, and he grinned.

"Hellooo…"

Zeke snapped his head around to Chad. "Sorry, buddy."

Chad shook his head sadly. "Dude, you are so whipped."

He frowned. "N-no, I'm not."

"You look at her as if she hung the moon."

Zeke shrugged uncomfortably, not so sure that she hadn't. "I'm enjoying b-b-being with her. A l-lot, actually."

Chad had his head cocked to the side and a funny look on his face. "Do you love her?"

For a long moment, he couldn't answer, because his heart clutched in his chest. "Yeah, I think I do."

"What did she say when you told her about the surgery? She'll be there, right?"

Zeke looked away from his best friend's face. "I d-d-didn't tell her."

"What? Why the hell not?"

"Because sh-sh-she's been through a l-l-lot this week. I'm not going to freak her out by r-r-r-, telling her all the damn statistics about the dangers involved with this one. I'll tell her when I'm in recovery and I've made it through. Assuming she even sticks around."

Chad shook his head sadly. "Dude, you're going about this wrong. She'd going to be so pissed at you."

Zeke shifted uncomfortably, second thinking his decision. "I-if I tell her now, all sh-she'll do is w-w-worry. And if she sticks around afterwards, maybe I actually mean something to her."

Chad seemed unconvinced, shaking his head from side to side. Zeke didn't like disappointing his buddy, but he felt strongly about this. He didn't know if she felt the same way he did. They'd only been hanging out for a few days. He *thought* he meant something to her. If he threw her into the deep end of his recovery, though, she'd probably bug out, just like he'd seen many other women do when they couldn't handle their soldiers' trials. "You can call her when I make it out. I'll give you her number."

Frowning, Chad didn't argue with him any more, but Zeke could tell he'd disappointed him.

EMBER WATCHED THE two men talking and wondered what put that irritated look on each of their faces. Zeke looked stubborn, with his heavy arms crossed and jaw clenched. She'd never seen him look so...unyielding. Chad looked up and caught her gaze, then looked away guiltily.

Hm. What wasn't Zeke telling him?

She debated crossing the room, then thought not. Chad had asked to speak to Zeke privately. Maybe it didn't even concern her.

She glanced at Shannon. The Grinch had rolled over in his wheelchair to ask her a question, and there was such a connection in the look they shared. As if the room could fall away around them and they wouldn't even notice. The man seemed so intense, dark eyes flaring with emotion when he looked at her. Shannon seemed to relish his attention. They were obviously very much in love. When Palmer rolled away, Shannon's eyes followed him until he disappeared into the kitchen.

Ember couldn't help but admire what they had.

"How long have you guys been together?" she asked.

Shannon glanced at her and grinned. "Not nearly long enough," she laughed. "Sorry. We've officially been a couple about two months, but I've been mooning over him for a lot longer than that."

Ember laughed along with her. "You guys seem to fit very well. I thought you'd been together longer."

"Nope," Shannon sighed, "we've just been through a lot of crap in a short amount of time." She waved her hand as if it weren't important. "Tell me about you and Zeke."

Ember shrugged uncomfortably. "He's been coming into the grill I run with my dad in the Flat Irons Mall area, and he caught my eye. I've been dealing with some crap, myself," she waved a hand at her fading bruises, "and he stepped in to help Drew and I out."

"Ah, yeah, the Marine thing," she gave her a knowing smile. "You might as well get used to it now because he'll never change."

Shannon was a great listener, and within no time Ember had poured out the entire story, and how they were dealing with the fallout this week.

"You did what you needed to do," Shannon said finally. "You can't mess with PTSD. We've heard too many stories about how quickly the whole situation can go bad. I bet your father's buddy who committed suicide had untreated PTSD."

Ember sank back against the couch, propping her arm on the back. "You're probably right. I never thought about it to make the connection."

"The government has gotten better about recognizing it and treating it, but they're so understaffed right now that there's a backlog of service men waiting to get the help they need." She shook her head, making the bell on her hat tinkle. "It's very sad."

Ember agreed, and hoped her dad actively took part in the treatment and appreciated the result.

Palmer rolled into the room with her son on his lap. Drew concentrated on holding a little gray cat in his arms and didn't look up until they stopped at the couch.

"Mom, look! Guess what her name is? Gray Cat. This is John's cat but he said I could hold her."

Shannon grinned as she looked at the man over Drew's head. "He said the cat was his, huh?"

Palmer winked at her.

Ember urged her son down. "Let me see."

The kitten didn't care who held her and loved being the center of attention. She was bigger than kitten size but not quite full grown. "Gray Cat, huh?"

Shannon directed a raised-eyebrow look at the Grinch, who scowled. "What? She likes her name. It's easy to remember."

Drew looked at John and nodded his dark head. "That's what I would have named her, too."

They all laughed.

Ember appreciated being included in such a great group of people. Zeke joked around with his buddies and seemed more relaxed than ever. When Shannon stepped away to greet someone at the door, Ember walked across to Zeke. He was talking to a more mature, muscular man with short gray hair near the fireplace.

"Ember, this is Duncan Wilde. The man who create LNF."

Ember shook the man's hand, excited to meet him. "Zeke has said wonderful things about you and the company. What a wonderful environment you've created." She made a motion at the men standing and sitting around them, laughing and joking.

Duncan looked around with a nod, but seemed a little sad. "It was needed. It's very nice to meet you as well, Ember."

When they walked out John and Shannon's door that night, she felt very content and more secure in her relationship with Zeke. He'd taken a chance by bringing her to the party. She kind of felt it had been a test to see how she reacted to the men and their injuries. Or something. She wasn't sure exactly.

Zeke carried a snoozing Drew out to the truck and buckled him into the seat. Ember's throat tightened with emotion as she watched the big man manipulate the straps carefully over her son. Then he held the door open for her to climb in. She slid across the seat but turned to face him. Zeke climbed in and started the truck, letting it warm.

"I wanted you to know," she whispered, "that I

loved meeting the people you work with."

He smiled at her. "They're more than just p-p-people I work with. They're my friends and family."

"I can see that," she nodded. "You're lucky to have that with your actual family so far away."

He nodded and scraped his hand through his hair. "I need to go back to see them. It's just hard being under sc-ru-ru-ru...they watch me like a hawk. And it makes me more nervous."

She raised a brow. "You may have to tell them that."

He frowned, adjusting the heater vents. He pulled a post-it note pad and pen from the dash cubby. "It's easier just not to deal with it, sometimes."

"Granted, but it's your family. Whether you like it or not."

He scribbled a note on the post-it sheet and dug his wallet from his back pocket. She watched him place the note in the center of the fold, on top of a stack of older notes. He glanced up at her and shrugged. "I have to keep track of words that give me trouble. When I go to my counseling sessions, we go over the words. Most of the time I can see them and hear them in my brain perfectly, know what they mean, I just can't spit it out."

"Wow. Do the doctors know why not?"

He shrugged and put his wallet away. "Something got screwed up in my brain."

Shifting into gear, he pulled away from he house. Ember stretched the seat belt across her body and snicked it shut. "Shannon is awesome. And John is hilarious. They suit each other very well."

Zeke shook his head, laughing. "They haven't been a c-couple very long. John was a...n-not very happy guy a few months ago, but Shannon has really ch-chilled him out."

"They just needed to find each other."

"Apparently."

The drive back to Ember's apartment was quiet and companionable. Zeke parked and carried Drew inside for her. They pulled his boots and jacket off, then she directed him to just lay the child in his bed. It was a little early for bedtime, but he was obviously worn out. Too many hours chasing Gray Cat.

Ember thought they were just going to relax, but when Zeke came out of Drew's bedroom, he made his excuses and headed to the door. Ember was a little hurt. They'd just had a wonderful afternoon, and she'd been looking forward to an even better evening, but apparently not.

Zeke pressed a lingering kiss to her lips and backed through the doorway. "I'll call you."

Ember waved a hand, at a loss as to what she'd done to chase him off so fast.

Well, I was pretty clingy. But then, he had been too. He'd never let go of her until Chad had asked to talk. Maybe he just had to regroup and figure some things out.

SHANNON SIGHED HAPPILY as she crawled into bed that

night. The party had gone wonderfully. No stress, just a group of friends getting together to celebrate the holiday.

John's wheels squeaked into the room. "Everything's locked up. That damn cat was curled up in the hallway closet, underneath a coat. I wouldn't have known if I didn't see her tail sticking out."

"Probably recovering after all the excitement," she laughed. Rolling up onto her side, she watched as he undressed. "Ember's little boy carried her around for hours."

John nodded and rolled into the bathroom.

"What did you think of Ember?" he called out.

"I think she was very nice. Calm and put together. It was her father who gave her those bruises."

John backed into the doorway enough to see her. "Are you serious?"

She nodded. "She filed charges, though, and he's going to get the counseling that he needs. He was a Marine in Vietnam."

John scowled and disappeared into the bathroom again. She heard water running and splashing in the sink, and her body began to warm. He would be crawling in beside her in a minute, and she could do with him as she pleased.

He rolled into the room and hoisted himself up into the bed. Shannon had offered to get a lower bed when he moved in, but he'd refused. She was glad, because it allowed her to watch the interplay of his substantial six-pack every night as he came to her.

She shifted over to give him room to stretch, then

curled in against him with her hand over his belly.

"Zeke will watch over her now."

She nodded against him. "Did you see them looking at each other? It was almost electric. And she only had eyes for him."

John's long arm coasted down her side beneath the comforter. "And he looked like he couldn't believe she was with him. I think the big man has fallen."

"Hard," she whispered. Her hand slipped down past his waist, but he stopped her.

"Hold on. I have one more gift for you to open."

Shannon peered up at his face in the dim light. "You already got me too many things."

John snorted. "I didn't get you shit. Just trinket things because I didn't know what else to get you."

"But I loved them. You got my favorite perfume, and I love the purse."

She felt him reaching at the side of the bed. He pulled out a little folded packet and held it out to her. Shannon sat up, crossing her legs, hooking the comforter around her shoulders. "What is it?"

He shoved it at her. "Just open it."

Shannon couldn't make sense of what it was at first. "Plane tickets?"

John rolled up onto his side, propping his head with his hand.

"To Cancun?" she gasped. She reread the papers over again, unable to contain a squeal. "Are you serious? A beach in the wintertime? Oh, John."

She bumped her head on his hard chin when she

pounced on him, but she didn't care. He shifted to his back as she peppered him with kisses and straddled his hips.

"I guess you like the idea, huh?" he chuckled beneath her.

Shannon paused long enough to look him in the eyes. "I love the idea. And I love you. More and more every day. Thank you."

She rocked her hips against his length and was rewarded when he went hard beneath her. "When do we leave?" she whispered.

"Uh, next week."

"Mm, just enough time," she gasped as she guided him inside.

SATURDAY EMBER TOOK Drew to Ms. Miller's house and headed into work early. It was a busy day. Deliveries were coming in and the crowds were out with the after-Christmas returns and sales. She hadn't heard from her dad, so she assumed he wouldn't be in yet. Which was fine. He had stuff to work through, too.

Two of the afternoon shift girls called off. Ember sighed as she listened to the second girl, Brandy, cry about her broken down car. "If you get it fixed, come in. We're slammed."

She hung up on a sniffle. She had no time for their crap.

The grill was packed, with a thirty minute wait for a

table. Ember worked harder than she had in a long time to keep things running smoothly, but she did try to step back and manage more. The wait staff seemed to appreciate the guidance, which surprised her.

At six o'clock, her dad walked in from the back. Ember whooped, joined by the rest of the staff, when they realized who was pulling the bar apron around his hips. Her father waved, a little embarrassed, but smiling nonetheless. She couldn't resist walking behind the bar and giving him a big, smooching kiss on the cheek. "So glad to see you, Dad."

"You know, I'm glad to be here. I thought you would be busy tonight."

He settled back into his rhythm quickly, pulling beers from the tap and chatting it up with every soldier that took the time to talk to him.

Ember watched the clock hands anxiously. Seven o'clock approached, and she watched the door as much as she could. But no dirty blond head appeared towering over the others. None of the other guys showed either. She owed them beer, so it was curious that they didn't appear.

As eight o'clock rolled past, she lost hope that they were coming. She checked her phone for the millionth time and found a text message.

Grill was jam packed, so we headed to Chad's. You be home later?

Yes! By 10.

See you there.

Ember was relieved they'd at least been here. She

should have left word with the hostess to get them in, but in the rush it hadn't even entered her mind.

She left the grill in her father's hands and climbed in her cold car for the fifteen minute drive home. Zeke climbed out of his truck and met her at the sidewalk when she got home, warming her from the inside out. Snow swirled around them as he pulled her into his arms for a desperate kiss.

Ember looked up at him in concern when he eventually pulled away. "Are you okay?"

He nodded and walked with her to retrieve Drew. The boy was asleep on Erin's couch, but woke when they shook him.

"Hey, Zeke."

"Hey, buddy."

As Zeke steadied him, Ember slid the boy's coat on, fastening the hood over his head. Snow boots next. The big man then lifted him into his arms.

"Thanks, Erin."

Ember rushed ahead to open the door for her boys. Zeke kicked off his shoes when he came in, then padded through the apartment to Drew's room, and they reversed the process. While Zeke steadied him, Ember took off his coat and boots.

Drew's eyes never opened the entire time, but he did smile when they tucked him into bed, pulling the covers up to his chin. "Night, guys."

Ember laughed. He was already out.

She returned to the living room to take off her coat, and draped Zeke's over the chair. "I'm sorry it was so crowded tonight. If I had known you were there I would have tried to get you in."

He shrugged as he settled on the couch, his look somber. "I don't know that we could have come in anyway. Diego saw the people inside and damn near had an anxiety attack right there at your front door."

Ember cringed, feeling bad for the Hispanic man. He'd been a real sweetheart when he'd helped her move in. "That must be so hard."

Zeke turned up his hands. "For the most part you get used to it. People stare at me all the time. Diego's going to take a while though. He was shot by an Afghani policeman he was training. One of our allies. In a group of people."

"No way. Seriously?"

Zeke nodded.

That just seemed so wrong. And sad. Disheartening.

Ember leaned into him and he wrapped his arm around her shoulder, pulling her into his side. Even though it was cool in the apartment, his burning warmth seeped into her. "You feel so good to me," she sighed. She tightened her arm across his lean middle.

Zeke pressed a kiss to the top of her head. "Hey, I, uh, need to go away for a few days."

She pulled back enough to look at him. "Okay...For work?"

He frowned. "Kind of, yes."

She felt like he was hiding something, but she didn't know what. "Okay. I'll be here when you get back. Can you call me?"

He shook his head. "At least not for a couple days. I will when I can."

"Is it dangerous?"

His look darkened and he squeezed her hand. "Yes, but I p-p-promise I will do my best to stay safe."

That sounded true enough, but even if he was lying did she have the right to call him on it? They were sleeping together, but he hadn't even hinted at anything more permanent. Ember knew she was in love, but she had a feeling if she told him it would spook him.

"You do that," she murmured, leaning into him tighter.

Zeke kissed the top of her head. Ember turned her face up and he pressed his lips to hers. She opened her mouth to his seeking tongue and was swept away by the desperation and need she felt in his movements. Pushing from the couch, he tugged her to stand, then swung her up into his arms to carry her to the bedroom.

Ember felt cherished. And feminine. Protected. He was so obviously male, layered with muscle, and he felt like her champion, her hero.

When he dropped her feet to the floor, he started working on her clothes. He didn't move fast enough, so she stripped her jeans and long-sleeved shirt away, tossing them to the corner. He stripped himself down and pressed her to the mattress, climbing between her thighs. Ember moaned as he slid against her heat.

"I need in you."

She widened the cradle of her hips and tilted up, reaching down with one hand to guide him into her body. Though he hadn't worked her like he normally did, she was still ready, because she'd been thinking of loving him for hours. As soon as he had texted her at the grill, she'd hoped this was how her night would end. She squeezed along his length.

As he began to lunge into her, she felt complete. This was where she was supposed to be and Zeke was the one she was supposed to be with.

All of the trials of their lives narrowed down to just his body gliding into hers, the desperation feeding their movements. They were both running toward that pinnacle of pleasure.

She found hers first, the head of his heavy cock gliding over the bundle of nerves to the front of her pelvic bone. As she bit into his neck and arched beneath him, crying out, Zeke lifted her hips in his hands, stroking her all the harder in the pursuit of his own pleasure.

Ember was lost in a daze of sublime sensation, quaking with aftershocks. "I love you," she sighed.

Zeke stalled out above her, quivering. "W-what?"

Hell. She hadn't meant to say it out loud, but now that she had… "I love you."

The echo of her words still hung in the air when he ejaculated. A long, loud groan poured from his throat as his body climaxed above her, shoving himself as deep as he could go inside her. Ember felt every jet of release deep in her womb, and her body quaked with another release in reaction. She gasped, trying to drag oxygen into her shuddering body.

"Oh, fuck," he sagged into her, but tried to brace the bulk of his weight with his elbows.

Ember wriggled beneath him, loving the contact. "You're not too heavy."

He relaxed a little bit, but not all the way. Leaning over onto one side, he looked at her in the dim light from the bathroom. "D-did you m-m-mean it?"

She smiled at the nerves she heard in his deep voice. "I did."

"Tell me again," he demanded.

Zeke held her all through the night, only moving enough to love her again, before asking her to tell him again. If Ember had been a less strong woman, she'd be worried that he wasn't reciprocating the sentiment. But she understood that it would take a while to reset the belief that he was unlovable because of his scars. When he woke her the next time, she rolled him to his back and proceeded to kiss her way across every scar on his head, then she moved down the breadth of his body.

Just before she drifted off to sleep in the early hours of the morning, he stroked his hand over her hair. "Thank you, Ember."

CHAPTER NINE

ZEKE CREPT OUT early the next morning, before either Drew or Ember had woken. As he sat in his truck, waiting for the damn thing to warm up, he shook his head. Who would have ever thought he'd be in this predicament.

Ember could, quite literally, drop him to his knees. If she looked at him with those soulful, dark chocolate eyes, he'd do anything for her. And tell her anything. That was why he had to get out of the apartment. If he didn't, he was going to beg her to go to the hospital with him in the morning. That wouldn't be fair to her.

Zeke prided himself on being self-sufficient. Chad had called him pussy-whipped. Maybe he was, hell. He just wanted her beside him. End of story.

When he got home, he crashed. He was scheduled for surgery at seven am, so the longer he could sleep up until that time, the better.

Chad picked him up at four am the next morning, looking bleary eyed but solid. He grinned at Zeke, and shook his head. "What the hell are we going to do when you get all purty?"

Shaking his head, he snorted. "I have a l-l-long ways to go until then."

They didn't say much on the drive south to Colorado Springs, but then, they'd done it several times before. They walked into the doors of the hospital at five thirty, an hour and a half before the scheduled surgery. A chatty nurse checked him in and took his vitals, then parked him in the waiting room to wait for an escort.

Zeke worried his thumbs back and forth over each other and fought the nausea in his stomach. This was surgery number thirteen. He should be used to baring himself for everybody to see by now, but it was still an effort to keep his ass parked in the chair.

An orderly called out his name.

Handing his cell phone to his buddy, he fought not to look at the display one more time. Ember had sent him an 'I love you' last night that made his heart stutter in his chest. "Her number is in there, but you can't call her until I'm out of surgery."

Chad nodded and powered down the device, pocketing it along with his own. "I'll take care of it. Don't worry about anything, just keep breathing on that table. You get me?"

He nodded and accepted a back pounding hug from his buddy. "I will."

"I'll be in the recovery room when you get there."

The orderly waited patiently at the open steel doors. With a final nod, Zeke forced his boots in that direction.

A SMILE SPREAD her mouth as she saw Zeke's number

on the phone display. She dried her hand on the bar rag. "Hey, sexy man. I didn't think you'd be able to call for a few days."

"Uh, Ember," a man cleared his voice. "This is Chad."

A wave of fear trickled through her. "Chad. Why are you on Zeke's phone? Is he okay?"

"Well," the other man hesitated. "Not exactly. We came down to Colorado Springs for surgery and it didn't go exactly right."

"Surgery?" Her head swam. "I thought he was on a job somewhere."

His boss sighed at the other end of the line. "No, he told you that so that you wouldn't worry. He was supposed to have reconstruction today, but something went wrong."

Her mind was reeling, and she dropped to her ass in a chair in the middle of the restaurant. "What?"

He sighed again. "I think you should come down. We're in Colorado Springs. I'm sending somebody to pick you up and drive you, okay? We've made arrangements for your son, but he needs a bag. Your ride will be there in an hour, okay? Are you listening?"

She nodded. As if he could see.

"If Zeke's as important to you as I think, you need to come down."

"Of course he is," she snapped. "I'll be waiting."

She debated whether or not to even talk to Drew, but she had a feeling he would want to know. He cried a little bit, then gave her a big hug and told her to go take care of him. She talked to Erin for a few minutes and explained that he would be gone for a few days, but that she was passing along Erin's info in case they needed her help.

It felt surreal unlocking her apartment and looking for overnight bags in the mess of her closet. But she did. She packed enough for three nights, just in case. She packed extra clothes for Drew, knowing he tended to be messy.

She changed out of her uniform and hopped in the shower for a super-quick rinse off. Shudders attacked her as she stood under the steaming water, but she didn't allow them to consume her. She stepped out of the shower, toweled off and dressed over cold, damp skin. Taking a few precious minutes, she blew her hair dry, then dragged it into one thick braid to hang down her back.

When the knock sounded on her apartment door, she was ready, bag in hand. Duncan Wilde himself stood on the other side, hip cocked against a cane. John Palmer sat in his wheelchair beside him. He rolled forward.

"Shannon and I are going to take Drew if that's okay with you. We have an extra bedroom and plenty of room."

Ember nodded, not hesitating for a moment. Drew would probably love staying with them. "Thank you."

The little boy was ecstatic and barely said goodbye to Ember as he went through the door, riding on John's lap. Duncan looked at her, brows raised. "Are you ready?"

Ember snatched up her own bag, slid on her coat and locked the door.

It was a very quiet ride to Colorado Springs, broken only by the rhythmic thumping of the interstate beneath them. Afternoon traffic slowed them down, but only for a few minutes.

"You knew, obviously, he was going in for surgery. Did everybody know?"

Duncan shook his head. "Just his immediate supervisors."

Ember felt so very hurt. Why on earth hadn't he told her what was going on? She'd have been there right beside him the entire time. "Why didn't he tell me?" She hated the touch of whine in her voice.

Duncan shrugged, turning the wipers on to get rid of the few flakes falling. "I'm not sure. Maybe he didn't think you could deal with it."

She frowned, offended. "Seriously?"

Duncan sighed and shifted in his seat. "Seriously. A lot of people, mostly women, can't deal with their significant others' long-term care issues. This may be TMI, but my fiancee left me bedridden in the hospital years ago when I returned from Iraq. At the time, she thought I was going to be in a wheelchair the rest of my life."

Ember blinked, deflating. "Oh, wow. I'm so sorry to hear that."

He flashed her a smile. "It turned out okay. But you may want to cut Zeke some slack. He was already under a lot of stress about the surgery."

"What exactly did he go in for?"

"Some reconstruction of his forehead area. Minimize some of the scarring."

She sat back in the seat, thoughts chasing through her head. If she pushed the hurt aside, she could understand his reasoning. Hell, they'd been together barely more than a week. She recounted the days, just to be sure, but it was true. It just felt like they'd been together longer. They'd traveled a lot of emotional ground in that time.

Was she bothered by the thought of more surgeries down the road? Well, yes, but only because of the potential threat to his welfare, not because she didn't want to be there with him.

She loved him. It was that simple.

Actually, she was irritated he'd gone and changed *his* face without telling her. She'd grown very fond of it over the past several weeks.

When they parked at the hospital, she followed Duncan inside to the elevator bank. He seemed to know where he was going. "Were you here with him when he went in?"

He shook his gray head. "No, Chad came down with him. He's been in here before for the same thing several times, though, so I know where to go." He glanced at her. "I need you to go along with what I say in a minute, okay?"

Ember nodded, curious.

The elevator took off. When the doors slid open, Duncan led her around to the right, through an automatic set of double doors, past a nurses' station and then around another corner to a second nurses' station. He stopped and smiled at the dark-haired woman behind the counter. "This is Ember Norton, Zeke Foster's fiancee. Has there been any change in his condition?"

The woman smiled and dug a chart from the pile in front of her. "The doctor is in there now if you want to step in."

Duncan wrapped his hand around her elbow and tugged. She was still dazed from the fiancee bit, but she got her feet untangled and moving.

"I can't take you in there without warning you that there will be a lot of stuff on him. Bandages, IV, I'm sure. Don't freak."

She nodded, appreciating that he kept hold of her arm. "Okay."

He slowed at a door on the left, then pushed through, pulling her along with him. A man in a white coat blocked the doorway talking to Chad, and she couldn't immediately see Zeke. She pushed past the obstruction, then stopped. Tears came to her eyes as she finally saw him.

Stretching the length of the hospital bed, her big, strapping warrior was out cold. A clear oxygen mask was tight to the only part of his face not covered. From the jaw up on the left side, his head was wrapped in a beige mask.

She stepped to the side of his bed and reached for his hand, shocked at how cold his big fingers were. She wanted to lean down and kiss him, but there was nowhere she could touch without fearing she would hurt him. The back of his hand had a clear IV in it, and was taped up his forearm. There was an oximeter on one of his fingers to measure oxygen in his blood. He had a blood pressure cuff encircling his other arm.

Ember looked to the doctor she'd pushed out of the way. "Is he okay?"

The man didn't seem put out in any way and smiled at her. "He is. In spite of his appearance. We had a few issues during surgery, but he seems to be recovering well."

Duncan leaned in, brows drawn. "What kind of issues?"

The doctor shifted on his loafers and flipped open the chart in his hand. "Well, the resident responsible for one portion of the surgery nicked an artery, and we had a bit of a bleeding issue."

"I overheard one of the nurses talking and she said it was a lot of blood." Chad had his arms crossed, and Ember was surprised to hear anger lacing his voice.

"Not a lot," the doctor held up a placating hand, "but a good amount. The arterial repair didn't want to hold and we had to call in a vascular surgeon to transfuse him with a couple pints of blood."

"A couple?" Duncan's dark eyes narrowed on the man. "How many exactly, Doctor?"

The harried man looked down at the chart in his hand. "It looks like we needed three pints when all was said and done."

From the look on Chad and Duncan's faces, that was

a lot.

"Is he okay now?" she asked, heart in her throat.

The doctor nodded. "We were able to repair the artery and completed for now the repairs to the previous facial scarring we wanted to do. He's right on track with his post-op recovery plan. As soon as he wakes up from the anesthesia, we'll settle him in a room. Barring infection, he should be out of here within a few days."

The knot of tension in the middle of her chest eased a bit, and she took a deep breath. "When will he wake from the anesthesia?"

The doctor gave her a look. "Well, technically, he should have been awake by now. He's taking a little longer than normal. But, his body's been through a lot of insults and shock trauma today, and sometimes the body and mind knows better than we do when to surface. Just press the nurse button when he opens his eyes."

The doctor made his escape then, and Duncan shut the door firmly behind him. "I have a feeling we aren't hearing everything."

Chad nodded. "The nurse I heard said that it was pretty touch and go there for a while, and his bp had bottomed out."

"How much blood does the average person have in their body?" she asked.

Chad and Duncan shared a look, as if they didn't want to tell her.

"Six or seven pints. Maybe eight for a guy Zeke's size," Duncan told her.

Ember cringed at the thought that he had lost so

much blood, from a tiny, misplaced slice.

"Does this happen every time he comes in?"

Chad shook his head. "Definitely not. Never had any problem like this before. I've been with him for two of these since he's been with the agency."

Ember watched the even rise of his chest under the blue gown. It seemed steady. Watching his face, though, his eyelids didn't even flicker. She ran her hand over his shoulder and the upper part of his chest, anxious to feel something.

Chad shifted a chair closer to the bed for her. "You might as well have a seat. It'll be a while."

Duncan left the room and when he returned a few minutes later, an orderly followed him in with two more chairs. The man positioned them then left.

Ember shook her head at the ease with which Zeke's boss got things done. "Does everybody do what you want them to do?"

Chad laughed out loud as he settled into one of the chairs. "Yes, if they know what's smart. Otherwise he'll pout like a baby and glare daggers at you until it's done."

Duncan raised a brow at Chad and shook his head. "Don't you have a piece of taffy to chew or something?"

The Texan unwrapped a piece of gum and tossed it in his mouth, grinning. He winked at Ember and leaned close. "Boss man thinks this'll shut me up. You'd think he'd know by now."

Ember laughed, appreciating that they were trying to lighten the mood for her.

They all three settled in to watch him breathe. About

two hours after they got there, he groaned, then his eyes began to roll back and forth beneath his eyelids.

Ember was at his side in an instant, leaning over the head of the bed to him.

When his dark lashed lids lifted, she made sure she was the first thing he saw. "Hey, beautiful. Can you hear me?"

He lifted the hand nearest to her and grabbed her forearm. Ember fumbled for the nurse's button through her tears.

As the hours passed into night and Zeke began to rouse more, she lost track of how many nurses and doctors trooped through the room, checking this and that. At one point they took off his oxygen mask and hung it on a hook behind the bed. He answered their questions in a painfully raspy voice.

One sweet-faced nurse brought him a jug of ice water, but cautioned him to drink it a little at a time. As soon as she left, he reached for the jug. Ember grabbed it and held the straw to his lips, but pulled it away after a few swallows. "You better take it slow," she cautioned.

Zeke looked at her and smiled. "I thought you'd be pissed at me."

She couldn't help but return his smile. "I am. But I'll wait to rip into you."

He snorted and squeezed her hand.

ZEKE DIDN'T KNOW what he'd done in his life to garner

such great friends. His gaze rested on Ember curled up in the chair beside him. And lovers.

When he'd opened his eyes and seen her standing over him, he'd thought it was the anesthesia messing with his head. He'd told Chad not to bring her in until he came around, but his buddy had obviously decided otherwise. When Duncan told him about the near miss he'd had, he'd been shook, and understood.

Complications during surgery were always a possibility, but nothing had ever happened before now. Figures, the one time it *needed* to go smoothly and it hadn't.

Shame had coated his stomach when he realized how bad he probably looked. Even though he couldn't see it, he felt the beige compression mask cinched around his neck and head, and everything not compressed was probably swollen. He remembered seeing himself in the mirror the first time like this, and it hadn't been pretty. Without it, though, his face felt like it was pulling apart. They gave him enough pain killer to take the edge off, but nothing completely took away the bone-deep ache.

She hadn't hesitated or flinched when she'd looked at him though, and the little flicker of hope that she could take this stuff flared a little brighter. Every time the doctors and nurses came in, she asked questions. Same stuff he'd asked through the years. Should it look like that? How long would it take to heal? How long did the stitches need to stay in? When could he resume normal activity?

The one time she did break, just a little, was when they removed the pressure bandage and she realized they'd shaved him. He raised a hand to rub over the stubble and old scars on his head in embarrassment. Her brown eyes got big and she slapped a hand over her open mouth.

"All that beautiful hair gone…"

…and all the hideous scars revealed.

The second part he heard screaming completely through his head. She hadn't said it, but she might as well have.

"…will make you look like a total bad-ass."

Zeke looked up at her with a frown, unsure he'd heard her correctly. "What?" he croaked.

"As if six and a half feet of Marine wasn't bad enough, now you have to look like an enforcer out of a movie or something."

Once again, it was like she'd just kicked his bouncy-red-dodgeball life on end and his reality had to shift to align with her reality. She didn't mind the scars. Emotion tightened his throat. As chickenshit as it would sound, he needed to hear the words. "You really don't mind them?"

She squinted at him as if he were out of his mind. "Seriously? Hell, no. Although Drew may start calling you Humpty Dumpty with your egg cracked like that."

Barking out a laugh, he'd tugged her hand to his mouth for a kiss to her palm. When that wasn't enough he forced her to lean over the side of the hospital bed so he could fold her into his arms.

Ember stayed by his side through everything, even when the guys went back to work. When they changed his bandages, she peered around the nurses shoulders to watch them do it. When they got him up to walk the floor, she tagged along. It was comforting, although a little strange, that she was right there all the time. He'd never imagined he could have that kind of support from anybody.

They talked about everything, from sports to guns to politics. The only thing they didn't talk about was the fact that he didn't tell her he was coming in here. It bugged him so much that two days after he woke he had to break the silence.

"So, the anticipation is k-k-killing me."

Ember looked up from the book she held open before her. Zeke muted the flatscreen hanging on the wall across from him.

"It's been two days and you haven't said a word."

She didn't need any clarification. "Because I know I'm probably going to yell, and I don't want to do that here."

"Well, can we talk about it without yelling?"

She sighed and set her book to the side.

"No, because I'll probably cry."

Zeke sighed, feeling like shit, wishing she was close enough to touch. "I didn't want you to worry."

"I know," she said. "But don't you think it was more traumatic for me to walk in here cold and see you like this? Or was that the test? To throw it all at me at once to see how I did?"

Zeke cringed, because that kind of had been his reasoning. He'd expected her to bail—had always expected her to bail—so he'd stacked the deck in that direction. "I'm sorry. That was a b-b-bonehead move on my part. You're right, though. What I go through is sh-shocking, and this isn't the end of it. I have several more...s-s-surgeries before I think I'll be able to walk out in public without feeling like a fr-reak. I wanted to be sure I could count on you before I fell any more in love."

Ember was shaking her dark head. "You're not a freak. Quit saying that. Wait, what?"

He swallowed, aware his brain had spit out what it was thinking rather than what he wanted to say.

Her dark chocolate eyes widened and she sat back in the chair as if she didn't believe what she'd heard. "In love? Did you really just say that?"

Zeke refused to take it back. "Yes, I did."

Ember, on the other hand, looked pissed. "You did this because you loved me."

He flinched, even though it hurt. "No..."

"What a freaking ridiculous..." she lunged to her feet, throwing her hands in the air, "senseless, egotistical Marine thing to do! All this protective, defensive bullshit has to stop. I won't stand for it. I told you flat out that I loved you. I think I loved you when you kicked those college kids out after they grabbed my ass. I know I loved you that day in my office when you held me in your arms as if you couldn't let me go and let me cry out my frustration. I love your looks, even though," she glared at him, "you went and changed them without telling me."

She shook her head and looked at the floor for a minute, before lifting tear-drenched eyes to his. "But your looks aren't why I love you. You're strong and resilient and have a heart of absolute gold, and I can tell when you touch me that you would walk over glass for me. Most especially, I love the way you treat my child, with respect and encouragement."

Zeke slid out of the bed to stand barefoot on the cold floor in front of her. "I would walk over g-glass for you, in a damn hospital gown with my ass h-hanging out. And your son is brilliant. I look forward to playing Legos with him again." He dared to reach out and tuck some hair behind her ear. "And I love you because you're the only one that sees me, not the scars or the h-history, just me. You scare the hell out of me with how much you see."

She grinned, tilting her mouth up for a kiss. "I do, huh?"

He kissed her carefully, yearning to sink into her more deeply. A nurse bustled in just then.

"Okay, now, that's enough of that," she laughed. "Let me check a couple things and I think the doctor is going to release you in the morning."

She urged him to sit on the side of the bed and started to carefully peel the stretchy mask away from skin. Ember stood just beyond the woman's shoulder, and he appreciated her being there. It seemed right.

He watched her face for any sign of disgust as the ragged, angry skin beneath the mask was revealed, but nothing appeared. She cringed and gasped in sympathy when one of the stitches caught, then seemed ready to beat the nurse, which made him snort.

"Do-don't make me laugh, damn it."

She winked at him over the nurse's shoulder and smooched him a kiss. Such a sense of calm descended through his body that the nurse could have ripped the mask away and he wouldn't have minded. He'd had brotherhood in the Marine Corp, solidarity, but he'd never felt it with another single person the way he did right now with Ember.

He waited until she met his gaze. "I do love you."

Her face eased and relaxed into a smile. "I love you, too."

"I want you and Drew to marry me."

The nurse lifted the mask completely from him, sniffed and tactfully left the room.

Ember's brown eyes were wide and luminous with tears. One slipped down her cheek. "And I can speak for Drew when I say we want to marry you too. He already told me you needed a family. Our family."

Emotion tightened his throat and made his eyes burn.

"I never e-e-expected to find somebody willing to take all of me, like this."

She shook her head and stepped between his knees, reaching for his hands. "I've told you before and I'll tell you a million times more. Your scars don't bother me. I love them, because they tell me exactly the kind of man you are, willing to fight for your country and your brothers. If you never have another surgery, I'll be fine with it. The outside isn't the important part to me. It's this right here." She laid her hand over his pounding heart.

His damn eyes. He wiped the tears away and pulled her into his arms. "I'll love you forever," he vowed. She tightened her arms around his neck and pressed kisses to his skin.

He cleared his throat. "I do need to talk to yo-your d-dad, though. I'm doing this b-b-backwards."

She nodded against him and pulled back to give him a watery smile. "He would appreciate that. And I would too."

THEY RELEASED HIM the next morning. As he and Ember walked out into the cold December day, he felt the stares of the people around him, but he didn't turn away from the scrutiny. He just looked down at Ember and smiled.

Chad had parked in the loop to wait for them. He stepped out and leaned against the front fender. His eyes tracked down to their clasped hands as they walked toward him, then back up to scan his face. Zeke grinned, even though it tugged sharply at his stitches and stopped in front of him. "I may need a b-best-man in the not-so-d-d-distant future."

Chad's eyes got big with surprise and he let out an "Oorah!", dragging him into a backslapping hug. Zeke laughed and took the assault, not caring that they were drawing more looks.

Then his buddy turned to Ember and wrapped his arms more carefully around her. He whispered something in her ear and she nodded. When they stepped apart, they were both teary eyed, making Zeke wonder what had been said.

Nodding his head, Chad turned to him. "I'll be there for you, Tiny."

Zeke laughed out loud and punched Chad on the shoulder, appreciating his life more than he had in many years.

THE END

FROM J.M. MADDEN

I sincerely hope you enjoyed Book 2 of the Lost and Found Series. I would appreciate it if you would:

LEND IT – to friends and family. It is lending enabled.

REVIEW IT – at the site you purchased it from.

RECOMMEND IT – to anybody you think would enjoy it. Positive reader reviews have a huge impact on the success of book.

About the Author

I am a wife and mother of two. I am a stay at home writer, which I dearly love, and I recently added the title USA Today Bestselling author to my moniker.

I was a Deputy Sheriff in Ohio for nine years, and I found myself tapping that experience as I wrote Second Time Around, my very first book. No, I didn't tackle and cuff my husband, although there was that time in K-mart… Anyway, it was quite a change going from writing technical reports with diagrams, witness statements, inventories, etc., that would stand up in court to writing contemporary romance. I've always written, though, and it was always a dream to do something with that huge, leaning stack of spiral bound notebooks.

I've now published 15 books, with many more on the way. I thank you so much for taking an interest in my work!

Stay tuned! There's a lot more coming!

Other Books by J.M. Madden

The Embattled Road (FREE prequel)
Embattled Hearts – Book 1
Embattled Minds – Book 2
Embattled Home – Book 3
SEALed with a Kiss Anthology
Her Forever Hero

Other books by J.M. Madden

Second Time Around
A Needful Heart
Wet Dream
Love On the Line – Book 1
Love On the Line – Book 2
The Awakening Society – FREE!
Tempt Me
Urban Moon Anthology

Connect with J.M. Madden

If you'd like to connect with me on social media and keep updated on my releases, try these links:

Newsletter

http://www.jmmadden.com/newsletter.htm

Website

http://www.jmmadden.com/

Facebook

https://www.facebook.com/jmmaddenauthor

Twitter

@authorjmmadden

And of course you can always email me at authorjmmadden@gmail.com

And now an unedited sneak peek of Embattled Home, Chad's book, out now!

Chapter One

CHAD WENT FROM reclining in his seat, debating whether or not to take off, to hyper aware as he heard a crash of glass and a muffled sound from inside. His gaze snapped to the little white house with black shutters he'd been watching for the past couple months, but everything was dark. What the hell had he heard?

He'd been sitting here for five hours, waiting for the woman's supposed indiscretions to show up, and all had been quiet. The little girl had gone to bed several hours ago, just like clockwork. Lora O'Neil, formerly Malone, had then puttered around the house, picking up toys and re-locking windows and doors.

She had locked the windows and doors four times now.

Fumbling the door handle with his bad hand, he jumped out of the car and started to cross the suburban street, the hairs on his neck prickling. He circled her gray minivan and paused. Nothing moved. It was after midnight on a Tuesday and every normal person in this quiet Denver suburb was in bed. The woman had been the only one moving around. She'd been pacing constantly.

For a second, he debated what to do. If he went up

to the house to investigate, he ran the chance of being exposed. The woman never slept for long stretches and as restless as she'd been there was a very good chance she was still up.

The decision was taken out of his hands when he heard a second crash from inside the house, followed by a woman's muffled scream. Adrenalin surged as he took off running. The front had been clear for the past several minutes, so he circled the house to the back door.

"Oh, shit," he grunted as he leapt the pile of glass that used to be her sliding glass door. Inside the house, things were upturned everywhere. Dark black potting soil littered the bright white carpet. The ceiling fan was swinging as if it had just been hit. His heart pounded as he saw a smear of blood on the opposite wall.

A thump from somewhere down the hallway guided his feet. What the hell was going on?

A second smear of blood told him he was in the right area as he cleared the doorway to the master bedroom. For several heartbeats in time he couldn't believe what he saw.

His client, the well-to-do, likable Mr. Derek Malone was beating the woman Chad had been hired to watch. Her left eye was already purple and swelling shut. Blood had begun to run down her forehead from a cut at her hairline. Derek had his hand clamped so tightly over her mouth he was pushing her head down into the mattress. Her clenched fists were beating at his head ineffectually, and Derek laughed as he reached for his fly with his other hand.

Chad was overcome with a violent fury.

Lunging forward, he slammed his right fist into the side of Derek Malone's face. The jerk never saw it coming. The force of the punch knocked the ass off the bed and against the wall, dazing him for a moment. When Derek looked up and saw Chad standing over him, he sneered.

"Get out of here, gimp. This doesn't concern you. It's between me and my wife."

"Ex-wife, asshole," the woman croaked from the bed, levering herself up. Chad was dismayed to see she was holding her right wrist, and her lip was split on the right side.

Chad's inattention cost him. Derek leapt up and sucker punched him in the right kidney, then tried a roundhouse to the jaw, but Chad jerked back just in time. Doubling his own fist, he smashed it up into pretty boy's nose, breaking it instantly. Blood gushed, and Derek crumpled back to the floor, his hands trying to staunch the flow.

"You son-of-a-bitch," he garbled. "You're fired."

Chad barked out a laugh and pulled his cellphone from his pocket. "Too late, dude. I already quit. LNF is off the case."

Dialing 911, he requested a squad car and ambulance.

"No siren," the woman pleaded. Nodding, Chad passed on the request and hung up. She was sitting up now, and Chad felt like shit. She was obviously in pain, hunched over and cradling her stomach and wrist. Occasionally she wiped away tears that coursed down her cheeks. At one point she found the blood on her head and sighed as she rubbed it away from her fingertips. Her whole demeanor screamed misery. It broke Chad's heart to watch her.

Derek, on the other hand, ran his mouth non-stop. Chad fought the urge to punch him again just to shut him up. When he started to berate the woman for being weak and asking for what he had done to her, Chad had had enough. Jerking Malone up by the collar, he frog-marched the shorter man out to the demolished living room to wait for the cops. He glanced at the woman before he cleared the doorway. "Will you be okay here alone for a few minutes?"

She nodded her head, wincing.

Within minutes, Denver P.D. arrived on scene. Chad flashed his state investigator's license and explained what had happened. Derek denied everything, of course, and told them he wanted his lawyer. They escorted him out in handcuffs, protesting the entire way.

The ambulance team had already disappeared into the back bedroom, and he found himself drawn back that way. The woman was blinking into a penlight beam with her one good eye and the paramedic was asking her questions. She looked up at Chad for a brief moment, and there was such desolation in her face that he almost stepped forward to console her. But he stopped when she looked away. It wasn't really his place to console her. Hell, he had been hired to gather evidence *against* her. Derek had retained the agency because he feared for his daughter's welfare, saying that Lora was subjecting the girl to unsavory characters.

So far, the only unsavory character he had seen her with was Derek.

Chad had collected no evidence the entire time he had been watching them. Lora kept her head down and watched everything warily. She hustled her daughter to and from the minivan and very rarely let her play outside. When she did go anywhere, it was to a nondescript house in Arvada where she would stay for several hours then leave. Chad had been unable to find out what was in the house, only that it was owned by a corporation. The only other person he had seen at the house had been an elderly black woman, no relation to Lora Malone.

Derek had said that he believed she had a boyfriend, and that she was partying at all hours, leaving her daughter to fend for herself. Derek's mother had also come forward with 'incriminating' evidence. Chad had a feeling now it had all been fabricated.

Chad had seen no evidence of any of it in the six weeks he'd been watching her.

"Is my mommy okay?"

Glancing down, Chad realized the little girl had come out of her own room, and was now peering into her mother's room. Shadowed green eyes widened when she saw the people grouped around the bed.

"Mommy?" her little voice quivered in fear.

"I'm okay, honey, just had an accident. Can you go to your room please?"

Chad's heart clenched when the woman smiled brightly for her little daughter. That had to hurt like a bitch with that split lip, but she didn't flinch at all. She was more concerned about reassuring her child.

Reaching down with his good hand, he turned the little girl's shoulders away from the doorway.

"Come on, sweets. Why don't you show me your room?"

Hanging her head, little Mercedes Malone trudged back into her bedroom. She dragged a stuffed animal with her by one ear. Chad realized it was supposed to be a dog, although it was about six different pastel colors. It was obviously well-loved.

Mercedes was supposedly six years old, but even to his inexperienced eye, the little one seemed tiny for her age. Climbing onto the twin bed, the little girl sat cross-legged in her pink and purple Dora PJs, not looking at Chad. Rumpled blond hair, so similar to her mother's, shaded her face.

"This is my room," she said quietly. "Is my mom okay?"

Chad looked at her in the illumination from the pale blue nightlight, debating how much to tell her. "I think she will be, but she has to go get checked by the doctors right now."

She blinked at him, and he frowned at the knowledge he could see in her eyes.

"She's had accidents before. But only when Derek's around."

It took everything Chad had not to flinch.

"Were you in an accident?" she whispered. "Is that why your arm is like that?"

He blinked at the shift in topic and looked down at the combat-modified appendage. "Yes, I was. Several years ago."

She nodded and lay down on her mattress, pulling the comforter over top of herself.

"Can't the doctors fix it?" she whispered.

He shook his head and looked at the bookcase beside him, desperate for a distraction. "Hey, this looks good."

He pulled out a white book with a little girl having tea with a group of stuffed animals on the front.

"Oh, that's my favorite," she sighed.

"Your mom must love you very much then, because you have a bunch of these books."

Chad realized that was the incontrovertible truth too. He had logged many man-hours watching Lora O'Neil, and he had never seen her raise her voice, let alone a hand, to the child. Quite the contrary, actually. The child seemed to have every toy a kid would need, and her room was outfitted with nice furniture. Many times he had watched Lora snatch the little girl up in her arms and give her big, tickling smooches, with Mercedes wiggling and giggling. He had only ever seen a mother who loved her child. Certainly not a woman endangering her daughter with her irresponsible lifestyle.

Chad had seen men approach Lora, attracted by her classic blond good looks. And he had seen them be shot down, one after another. Those unique forest green eyes would darken with contempt before she forced a smile, shook her head and turned away. It was a little depressing watching her go through as many men as she had, because he had to admit, she appealed to him as well.

Damn it.

He needed to call Duncan and let him know what was going on.

Chad began reading the book. It only took a few minutes for the little girl to slip back into sleep. Covering her a little tighter with the comforter, Chad replaced the book on the shelf and left the room.

In the other bedroom, Lora was arguing with the ambulance workers.

"I'm not going to the hospital. I can't."

"Ma'am, you probably have a concussion. I also believe you have cracked bones in your face. Judging by the swelling in your wrist, it could be broken too." The gray haired technician was obviously going over the same argument again. "You have to be seen by somebody."

Lora shook her head obstinately, even though it looked like it hurt. "I can't leave. I can't leave my daughter."

Chad fought with his sickening guilt. If he had been just a few seconds quicker, she never would have been hurt at all.

"I'll stay with her."

He didn't even realize he had spoken until she whipped a venomous glare on him.

"Oh, really? And snoop through my house and gather evidence on me? I heard what you guys said to each other."

"Then you heard me quit, too…" he told her quietly.

She frowned, trying to make sense of his actions. Chad gave her a hard look.

"You need to go to the hospital. If for no other reason than to have documentation when you take him to court."

Raising a bloody hand to her head, she shielded her eyes for several long moments, obviously weighing her options. When she eventually looked up at Chad, determination lined her face. "I'll call a neighbor to come over and sit with her. You don't need to. I'll go to the hospital in a bit, after the neighbor gets here."

The gray haired paramedic immediately started shaking his head. "Ma'am, you need to go now. With the swelling on your face, you probably have a concussion under there, which can lead to swelling and bleeding and eventually death. You need to be checked out by the doctors as soon as possible."

She seemed to understand the medic's warnings, because her shoulders slumped in defeat. "Okay, but not until she gets here."

Chad crossed behind the medic and picked up the cordless phone from the floor. One-handed, he pushed a button to silence the 'disconnected line' beeping and handed the receiver to her. "Call her now. I'll wait until she gets here so you can go."

The ex-Mrs. Malone was normally a beautiful woman. He had seen the professional photos and candid family shots the Malones had supplied, but right now she was a mess. Her blond hair was bedraggled and dirty, blood was streaked across her face, and her left eye was so swollen it would be days before it was back to normal. But she had a bearing to her that was indomitable. Her t-shirt was ripped at the collar and hanging down over one breast, but she sat on the edge of the bed as if she were wearing an evening gown. It was impressive, her courage.

Holding the cordless in front of her face awkwardly, she punched in several numbers. Whoever she called answered quickly and asked very few questions, because she clicked the off button within less than a minute.

"Heather will be here in about twenty minutes." Pointing a chipped-nailed finger at the nightstand, she motioned to a tablet and pen on one corner. "Write your name, cell phone number and who you work for on that paper, please. And your boss's contact number so I can call to confirm who you are."

Chad bent over the nightstand and wrote the requested information down. Then he wrote Duncan's cell phone number. What a cluster this night had turned out to be, and he still had to talk to his partner and explain what had gone down.

Even though it was after midnight Duncan apparently answered on the first ring, because the woman asked him questions like she was an attorney, one right after another. His partner seemed to answer everything to her satisfaction, because she handed the receiver to him. "Okay, you check out. He wants to talk to you."

Chad took the handset from her and motioned to the paramedic to get her on the gurney, because she looked ready to fall over on the bed.

"Yeah, Dunc?"

"What the fuck is going on over there? It was a simple surveillance op, gather info and that's it. No contact. What the hell happened?"

Stepping out of the room to give the medics room to carry her out, Chad leaned against a wall in the hallway. Lowering his voice so he wouldn't be overheard, he filled his partner in on the details. Duncan was quiet until he finished.

"Okay, Chad. I should have known you wouldn't go off like that without a reason. Is she going to be all right?"

"Yeah, I think so. She's pretty beat up. I'm glad I got here when I did though, because he was about to remind her of his conjugal rights."

"Shit," Duncan said softly.

"Yep." Chad stepped to the living room to watch as they hoisted Lora O'Neil into the waiting ambulance. Her eyes were closed and her head was tipped back against the cushion as if she were asleep. Chad would almost bet she would not allow herself to pass out. That was one strong woman.

Duncan was still speaking on the other end of the line and Chad had to look away from Lora. "What? Oh, yeah, I'm going to stay with the little girl until her friend gets here to watch her."

Leaning past the doorjamb, he peeked inside the girl's room. She was a lump under the covers, sleeping deeply. Chad nodded into the phone, following his boss's conversation even though he studied the child. "I will. I know. I know. Okay, see you tomorrow."

He stood in that doorway and watched the little one breathe. Twenty minutes later, a woman knocked softly on the front door before letting herself in. She showed him her identification. It matched up with what Lora had said to expect, so he let himself out the door.

LORA WAS IN a haze of pain. There was nothing on her that didn't hurt. And it seemed like the doctors were prodding every single injury just to grade her pain. 'So looking at this pain scale, how would you rate your discomfort?' She'd finally gone off on them. "It fucking hurts," she screamed.

The doctor had looked at her as if *she* were the one being unreasonable. After that, everything floated away on a cloud of pain medication. She didn't feel her sprained wrist being wrapped, and she didn't feel the needle in her scalp as they sewed in stitches. The light over the bed was a blinding source of aggravation, and it was a relief when they draped her face in the blue cloth in preparation of fixing her head. It shielded her eyes, and allowed her to rest for just a few minutes.

One of the nurses came in with a clipboard, asking if she had been the victim of sexual assault. Then didn't seem to believe her when she told her no. When she asked the same question for the third time, Lora finally just rolled over on her side and ignored the woman. She seemed to get the hint.

Sometime later, a Denver Police officer arrived to question her about the assault. Lora went through every detail she remembered, then told the woman about the voicemails she had been receiving on her phone. Mostly just hang-ups, but Derek had called yesterday to wish her happy anniversary, even though they had been divorced for two years. Lora had known then he would be coming after her.

No, he hadn't raped her this time.

The officer kept referring to the notes in her notepad, as if she already had a statement from somebody. Oh, yeah, the tall guy. Duh. He stayed until the squad had taken her away. He had apparently talked to the cops and told them what he had seen, too.

She didn't know what to think about him. Relief and appreciation that he had gotten Derek off her, but she was still royally pissed too. He'd been following her for weeks. Her paranoia had served her well when she'd spotted him at her work parking lot one day, and recognized him later on sitting down from the house when she went home. Had he actually thought she wouldn't see him? He followed her everywhere. Sometimes in different vehicles, but always about the same distance away.

What was up with that arm? It stuck out. Even in the midst of her own crises, she remembered cringing in shared pain for him. It looked like he had been burned or something. The flesh was eaten away, and the bones looked kind of warped, like the healing skin was pulling them into unnatural shapes. It looked painful. The scars spread all the way up his neck to his hairline behind his ear. There were a few scars on his face too, but they were just pale white lines, like they had happened several years ago.

It wasn't any business of hers though. She certainly had no reason to be worrying about his pain when she had plenty of her own.

The doctor, too young to have very much experience, admitted her. Lora had expected that and called the sitter to let her know. Truth be known, she dreaded letting her daughter see her this way. Mercy remembered hearing loud voices during the divorce, after Derek had found her, but Lora had carefully made up her face to cover any bruising she incurred. Between the shiner and the cut on her head and the bulky wrap on her arm, she was going to have a lot of explaining to do to her little girl.

They moved her to a quiet room on the fifth floor and finally dimmed the lights before leaving her alone. Lora tried to sleep, but the scene from her house kept replaying in her head. When she did doze off, she would snap awake at the slightest noise from outside in the hallway.

When there finally was a knock at her door, it was almost a relief to have a reason to sit up and be aware. "Come in."

The private investigator stuck his head inside and gave her a slight smile. "Mind if I step in for a minute, ma'am?"

All the anger of the night came rushing back. "Why? Do you need more pictures? Does he want proof of what he did?"

The man shook his head and held out both hands as

he stepped into the room. "No camera, I promise. And your ex didn't send me here. I came on my own."

"Why?" she snapped.

"I just wanted to check on you. I feel sick for letting you get hurt."

Lora took a moment to scan his somber face, and all she could see was truth in his vivid blue eyes. At least she thought he was being truthful. She wasn't a great judge of character recently. "I'm fine. It wasn't your fault."

He scrubbed a long hand over his short, walnut colored hair. "It was, though. I'd been there for hours, long past when I should have been off-duty, but something didn't feel right. I could tell you were nervous by the way you were acting and I should have been more aware."

Lora was torn. He seemed like a decent guy, just hired to do a job, but she was royally pissed he'd been watching her like that. "Well, I'm fine. I appreciate your stepping in when you did. Don't feel guilty about it. We're done."

For several long seconds he stared at her before glancing at the floor. When he looked back up, there was a determined look on his face. "Don't worry about our investigation. We are officially off the case. I talked to my partner and if there's anything you need us to do, please let us know." He fished a business card out of his wallet and stepped close enough to the bed to set it on the rolling table. "I called the jail. Derek will at least be kept for the night because they smelled alcohol on his breath, but it's up to the judge what happens in the morning."

Lora's insides tensed up when he stepped close, but she didn't let him see that. She stared at him as hard as she could with her good eye and left the card where it lay. "I don't believe I'll need your services."

Frowning, he turned away and crossed to the door. "That's fine, ma'am, but if he bothers you, let us know."

Lora didn't respond to his slow drawl and he walked out the door. She had a glimpse of scuffed gray cowboy boots before he disappeared.

Panic raced through her and she suddenly felt all vulnerable again. Her stomach shivered with fear, and she felt very alone sitting on the big bed. Slipping down off the mattress, she tried to drag the big recliner they kept for visitors over to the door with her good hand. It took her a while, but she eventually got it wedged underneath the handle. The nurses wouldn't appreciate it, but she would hear a person coming for several seconds. It would give her some time if she needed it.

After tugging on the locked window and crawling into bed, Lora finally allowed herself to relax. Emotions started to swamp her. Unfortunately, that also allowed the tears to come. *Five minutes, damn it, to cry. Then you're done.*

CHAD'S HEART ACHED in his chest when he heard the woman crying softly in the room. It tugged at his emotions, getting him choked up. He wanted to go back in and pull her into his arms and rock her until she stopped being fearful. The door was blockaded though.

And even if he made it in, she certainly wouldn't want his attention.

He gritted his teeth in frustration as he leaned against the wall. Lora O'Neil seemed to be a woman with heart, willing to fight for her child. Over the weeks he'd been watching her, Chad had found himself admiring her for her vigilance with their safety. The girl wasn't out of her sight at all, and the people that watched her seemed just as devoted. Lora worked at the local high school as a secretary, never missing a day or breaking her routine. It was why she'd been so easy to follow. He knew where she was going to be at all times. The only aberration was on Wednesdays, when she went to the big white house in Arvada. She would stay a few hours, then head home. Saturday mornings she took the girl to one of the parks in the city and then went grocery shopping.

The little girl would be worried when her mother wasn't there to cook her breakfast in the morning.

Walking down the hall, he talked to the nurse on duty. He was granted a little leeway with information when he flashed his investigator's badge. Lora would be released the next day at 11 o'clock, as long as the doctor thought she was able. Chad promised to be back then and headed out the door.

Embattled Home is out now!